*This book is dedicated to the amazing
Lauren Christopher,
Thank you for being my mentor and friend through this
very long, and sometimes tedious process. Without all of
your help, I wouldn't be where I am right now. All I
needed was to find that "happy meeting in between."
Thank you so much for helping me find that.*

"Sadie," Mom rocks me gently in my bed. I close my eyes tighter. Why would I want to go to school when there are so many other things I could be doing? "Come on, honey. It's time for school. Remember? First day of second grade?"
"My Barbies are going to miss me." I protest. "Why do I even need to go to school?"
"It's alright, Sadie. I know you don't want to, but it's important to learn new things. How about we go to Mason's Cakes for breakfast? You can get your favorite pancakes."
"Mason's Cakes!" I hop out of bed and put on my new flowery dress Momma got me for school. "I'm ready now! When do we leave? When do we leave?"
"No need to jump, Sadie. We'll be on our way now. Let's get your brothers. Come-"
Sprinting through the hallway, I throw open the door to my brothers' room. I crawl onto Mark's bunk first.
"Wakey wakey! Mason's Cakes time! Come on let's go!" I climb up the ladder to Peter's bunk next and start jumping on his bed. "Come onnnnnnn, slow poke!" Mom comes into the room just as I jump into her arms off of Peter's bed. "Nice catch, Momma!" I leap out of her arms and go to wake up Dadda.
Momma follows me through the hallway and waits as I burst into Dadda's room and leap onto his bed. No response. "Dadda? We're going to go get breakfast! Come on!" Still nothing from Dadda. "Are you there?" I throw back his covers. No Dadda. Where's Dadda?

I look through the doorway where Momma should've
been standing. Wait a minute. She's not there. I see a
shadow by the staircase. Maybe Momma wants to play
hide and seek. I run out of the room only to get stuck in
Mark's arms. "Let me goooooo!" I kick Mark in the no-
no square and run to where I saw Momma. Momma yells
from downstairs and I run to find her.
Yay! Dadda is here too! "Dadda! Come here!" I open my
arms for a hug but his hug feels different. I squirm a little.
He let's go quickly and turns to walk out the door.
"Momma?" I ask. "Where's Dadda going?" Momma
turns to face me and scoops me up in her arms. This time
I don't squirm.
"Dadda is gone, Sadie. I'm so sorry honey. Sometimes
there are things that you just can't understand when you
are little."
I look at Momma with tears in my eyes.
"Aunt Kara is going to come visit for a couple of weeks.
Isn't that exciting? She's your favorite person and wanted
to come be with us while we figure things out without
Dadda here. Don't worry Sadie, everything will be okay,
I promise."
I feel so confused. I don't know where Dadda went or
when I will see him again. We usually go visit Aunt
Kara in her super fancy apartment in New York, so it will
be nice to have her here for a change. I can't wait to see
her. I also feel scared about Dadda.
"C'mon, pancakes and second grade awaits you!"
Momma says, trying her best at a half smile.
Looks like this year is going to be so much different.

Chapter 1

Here I am again, in a tizzy trying to get ready for the first day of school. I run a brush through my long black hair and grab an AC/DC shirt and ripped jean shorts. I hear my mom preparing something in the kitchen as I burst down the stairs.

"Sadie, 10 minutes till the bus." Mom says as I make it down the stairs.

She hands me a bowl of cereal and I start gulfing it down, while at the same time still standing up. It wasn't my favorite first day of school breakfast, I think, comparing the soggy yellow cereal and green milk to my normal first day of school breakfast at my favorite café, Mason's Cakes.

"Why don't we ever go to Mason's Cakes anymore? It's been forever." I whine.

 I look up at my mom and she gives me a stern look. I sit down to eat breakfast and shut my mouth, just to please her. She gives me a softer face once I sit down but it immediately turns stern again once Paul enters the room. Her bright green eyes immediately turn dull just as mine do when I rip a seam on a piece of clothing. Mom doesn't even have to turn around to know its Paul entering.

"I'm off to work." Paul shouts as he starts running out the door.

"Get back here and say a proper goodbye." My mom yells, still not turning around to look at him.

He comes back inside and quickly kisses me on the forehead. Yuck.

"Where's Mark and Peter?" Paul asks, in a hurry.

"Don't know. Did they still not wake up yet?" Mom says.

"It was your job to wake them. I was up at 3 trying to call my client back. I told you to wake them."

"I didn't know. You expected me to hear you while I was asleep at 3 in the morning?" Paul says, starting to raise his voice.

I could feel the tension in the room. Why did they always fight about the littlest things? I honestly can't believe Mom is putting up with this jerk. I wouldn't stay with him even if it cost my family their house. Mom's trying to work as much as possible for her job that she hardly has time for other things. Since Mom's been in and out of jobs nonstop these last few years, she finally decided there was only one straw left to pull: She's remarrying to some super rich idiot, AKA Paul, so we can keep our home and get Mark and Peter to a good college. Sometimes, I feel like Mom might've actually found some love for him deep down inside. Although most of the time it's just bickering. I can't bear to hear the fighting between Paul and Mom so it's mostly just my brothers and I.

Mark and I look just like my mom with dark black hair and green eyes, while Peter looks slightly more like our dad with chocolate brown hair and hazel eyes. Dad has been pretty much out of the picture. We only saw him for court dates when I was seven years old. Eventually, Mom got full physical and legal custody of us and Dad left our lives forever. The only thing we ever see from him now are the child support checks for Mom.

Paul looks at me again and tries his best to give me a warm smile. He rushes out the door. No matter how hard he tries, he will *never* be anything close to a father for me.

Mom goes upstairs and wakes Mark and Peter while I finish scarfing down my food. The green milk in my bowl swirls around as I spin my spoon in the bowl. *Why is the milk so green?* I think. I go to the fridge and grab the jug of milk. I turn the jug around, looking at the designs. On one side of the jug, it has a picture of a cow that says "My land is your land. Freshly squeezed milk from the land down the lane." I flip the bottle around to the other side and look at the expiration date. It expired 2 months ago. When was the last time Mom went to the store?

As I close the fridge door with the milk jug in my hand, a flash of yellow catches my eye. I look down out the window and see the school bus turning onto the next street. I run out the door and try to catch the bus. The ground feels very hot for some reason, I notice as I sprint down the street. Then, I stop myself. I look down at my bare feet on the sidewalk. I sprint all the way back to my house. I set the milk jug on the counter, grab the shoes closest to the door, slide them on my feet, grab my lunch bag and backpack, and run out the door, again. *Take two.* I catch the bus stopping at a house a few blocks down. Three girls I don't recognize are getting on the bus, wearing clothes that look like they just got off the red carpet. As I get behind them to board the bus, the girl in the middle of the three turns and looks me up and down.

"You are?" she said, putting a finger to her chin like she's trying to remember me from somewhere.

I'm not sure I trust the girls so I talk with a slight, accidental, stutter. "S…Sa…Sadie. Sadie Benton." I try to smile but I'm sure it looks like a wolf about to attack its prey.

"Ok then, *Sadie*. I'm Brianna."

"Nice to meet you?" I say, sounding like it's a question.

"It's funny how it looks like you're using your brain."
The three girls laugh as they walk onto the bus. I walk on
behind them and find my friends Addy and Marie sitting
in the back. Addy laughs when I come up and sit in
between them. Marie has a sort of look of bewilderment.
"Hi." I say,
"Heyyyyyyyyy." Says Addy. "So…SPILL."
I slap my forehead. "Sorry. I completely forgot." Addy
challenged me to make it to the first day of school on
time, and properly dressed. If I didn't come on time and
properly dressed, I would have to wear her clothes for a
whole entire week. It's considered a threat when she
wants you to wear her clothes because:

    A. She never washes them
    B. She wears baggy clothes (Plenty of skulls included)
    C. All her clothes have at least three gigantic holes in
        them from either skateboarding, rock climbing or just
        her ripping them to be "cool"

"Do I really have to wear your clothes?"
"YES." She yells. Everyone turns their heads back to look at
us when I notice what everyone's wearing. Uniforms. The only
people not wearing them is that Brianna girl, the other two
girls, and me. I forgot. First day of middle school means
boring uniform.

"Marie?"
"Yes?" She answers, in her soft tone.
"Do you have a uniform I can borrow?"
"Of course. I always have a few spares." She pulls one
out of her bag and hands it to me.
"Thanks. How many do you have in there?" I say,
desperate to change the topic from me having to wear
Addy's clothes.

As Marie prattles on about how she brings a little bit of everything so she can get to know more people and become class president, my head drifts away to the world back home. Mom and Paul always fighting, or never home and Dad being completely absent for some of the biggest days of my life. Since Mark and Peter are seniors, Mark's dream of going to the military is becoming more real each day and Peter is about to get shipped away to college to get a degree, all in just a year's time. Meanwhile, my aunt is living it up in New York City with her designer clothing shop *and* a penthouse apartment. She's so lucky. *If I was old enough, I'd live in a big city. I'd be rich. I'd have-* "SADIE..." Addy's loud, booming, voice jolts me from my thoughts and I see that everyone is departing the bus. I get up and follow the other students off of the bus. As we walk onto school campus, I see the new principal greeting all the kids. As I try to walk past her as stealthily as possible, she notices me right away.

"You." she says, I stand up straighter and look at her. "Come here please." I walk towards her reluctantly.

"Why are you not wearing your uniform?" She asks.

"Sorry." I try to confess to her.

"Sorry does not fix anything. At this school, we show school spirit always. Now get in the bathroom and change. I can't have anyone see you in that…that…whatever you're wearing. Hurry along now. Classes are in 10 minutes."

What a warm welcome. I think. I start running to the bathroom when she taps me on the shoulder.

"No running please." She smiles brightly, too bright, it's sort of creepy.

I speed walk down the hall and into the bathroom. I change quickly and burst out of the bathroom a little too quickly and I crash into someone.

"Sorry." I say, looking down at my feet.
"It's alright." Says a nice, calming voice. I look up and
see a boy about my age with long, black, shiny, hair and
beautiful amber eyes. It seems as if for a second, I get lost
in them, so lost that my thoughts are sent back to my
house, but a better version of it. I have a dog, my mom
and Paul aren't fighting, my aunt and dad are there too.
We're all talking, eating steak that was grilled on what
looks like a new barbecue, an item my family could never
afford. I snap out of it and look down at my feet again.
"I best be going." I say, I walk slowly down the hall and
into my first class. All of a sudden, I feel like today is
going to be a better day.

Chapter 2

First period goes by like a breeze. Although no one I know is in the class, everyone is super nice to me. We learned some math and then did some reviews from last year. It was all fairly easy stuff considering how hard the older kids said the math teacher was. While everything in that class was great, my next class was a lot worse. PE. Brianna and the rest of her now growing posse came walking down into class 5 minutes late, not even wearing their PE outfits.

"Are you in this class?" Mrs. Carmelo, the PE teacher, asked them.

"Yes. We are. I need to mention something though. This dress was imported from Berlin and is made of the finest silk, imported from Milan. Sorry not sorry to say, but I won't be doing anything today that involves running, jumping, climbing, getting on the floor, getting on a bike, or anything else of the such." says Brianna.

"Excuse me?" says Mrs. Carmelo. "I believe I don't take orders from kids. Get in line because we're just about to start rope climbing."

The Brianna posse looks up at the twenty-foot-high rope hanging from the ceiling. Brianna's face dramatically changes and she looks like she's about to puke and then suddenly falls backwards, causing one of the boys in her posse to run up and catch her. Mrs. Carmelo slaps herself on the forehead.

"Leave her on the bench. When she gets up, she'll start with the warm up." Mrs. Carmelo instructed the boy who caught her. "As for you, I believe you'll climb the rope first because of your fast reflexes and strength." The boy froze in his spot by the bench where he set Brianna down.

"Come on then." Shouts Mrs. Carmelo, blowing her whistle. Brianna never ended up waking up until the bell for lunch rang. She sits up, jolts down the hall and into the lunch room, only to reserve a table for her and her posse. I sit down at the table farthest away from her group. I want exactly no part of anything to do with that stuck-up, spoiled, little, brat. Addy sits down next to me and Marie sits on the other side of the table across from the two of us. A few other kids fill up the empty spaces at our table and we all eat our lunches.

"How was PE?" Addy asks. "I have PE next period."

"Never better." I say sarcastically. I tell them everything that had happened using every little detail I could. I tell them about Brianna's red, silk, dress that was imported from Berlin or something. I then tell them about how she drastically fell over causing the poor, poor, mind controlled, boy into catching her, forcing him to climb the rope due to being late to the class and for his apparent strength. I continue telling them everything from the beginning of the day to right where we are now, leaving out the small part about the boy and his eyes that make you hallucinate things when you stare into them.

"Wow. What a day." Marie says in her soft, quiet, tone.

"So far. I still have 4 periods left. Praying it'll be better." I say.

We all get dismissed from lunch and head to our next classes. Mine history, Addy's PE, and Marie's math. As we head our separate directions to our classes, I see the boy again. I stop walking for a second to let him catch up to where I was. I walk over to him, my feet doing the exact opposite of what my brain told them to do, and say "Hi again. Sorry about earlier. I never got your name."

What am I doing? Class starts in three minutes.

"Oh. Hi. I'm Matthew Clint. What's your name?"

"I'm Sadie Benton. Nice to meet you."

"Yeah. You too. Are you going to history?"
"Yes." I say, "You?"
"Same here. Guess we can walk to class together?"
"Sure." I say. Honestly, that went a lot better than I expected considering the fact that my body did the moving and talking and not my brain. When we get to class, it appears that it already started. *Did I get lost in his eyes again? Did I misread the schedule?* However, none of these seemed to be the case. The teacher, Mr. Johnson, starts class early. I feel embarrassed and nervous and get that sudden rush of stage fright as everyone turns their heads to stare directly at me. It's not the first time I've been late to class, but this time I feel extra embarrassed. I look up at Matthew and we take our seats. We sit down at the only two empty seats left and sadly, I was stuck next to Brianna. She smirks at me and looks away. I try to focus on history but Brianna keeps scribbling something on her paper super loud and pointing at it. The girl on the other side of me pinches me.

"I think she wants you to look at that." I roll my eyes and try to take a brief look at the paper. Brianna's showing it to the other kids now so I look over her shoulder and see what it says. *Sadie's got a boyfriend.* I read. I know I shouldn't have freaked out because he wasn't my boyfriend, I just met him today. I reach over to her desk, snatch the paper out of her hand, and rip it to shreds. Her face does that dramatic change and she starts wailing, "Sadie ripped my paper. Mr. Johnson. Sadie took my paper out of my hand." Mr. Johnson turns around from the blackboard where he was working and stared straight at Brianna and I. Brianna always acts like a baby from what I've seen today. As Mr. Johnson turns his gaze to just me, I slump down in my chair. *I give up.*

"I'd like to speak to the two of you after class." he says. I focus the best I can during the rest of the class and head over to the teacher's desk afterwards. After all the rest of the class is dismissed, he turns to me.

"Where's the other girl?" He says, realizing Brianna's out the door. I shrug and he sits down in his desk chair. I start going through my head about what I'll say to him when he asks for an explanation.

"I don't know what to say about what happened except to not do whatever you did again."

I took a deep breath, starting to exhale my very detailed explanation when I realize what he said. "Really?" I say, in disbelief.

"Yes. I'm not taking anyone's sides today but if this behavior in class continues, I'll have another talk. You've been dismissed." I walk out the door and look at the big clock above the door. My next class started a minute ago. *Argh.* I pull out my map and run down the halls and into my next classroom, stealthily take a seat, and settle in for class.

Chapter 3

I plop down on the couch, Mark and Peter on either side of me, Mom on the other couch.

"Big day?" Mom asks. No one answers. "I see. How about I make you some hot chocolate?" She rushes off into the kitchen and leaves us to our thoughts.

"What's on your mind Sade?" Mark asks, calling me by my nickname.

"Nothing." I say,

"Come on. You can talk to us." Says Peter.

"I know, I know." They give me a look. "Fine."

 I tell them all about Brianna and the bus and my shoes. I tell them every last detail except everything about Matthew. Once again, I just don't feel ready to tell them yet. Why, though?

When Mom comes back in with the hot Chocolate, everyone drinks theirs slowly and talks a little bit more. When everyone finishes their coco, I run up to my room and pull out my mom's old sewing machine. I set it up on my desk, grab my fabric bin, and turn the machine on. I sit there thinking a little bit about what to sew as I look up at my inspiration board. *Nothing good.* I think. I go through my bin of fabrics next. Sequin? No. Lace? No. Linen? Definitely not. I keep digging through my bin till on the very bottom, I see a brownish-pink-with-hints-of-green-silk fabric. I hold it up in my hands to admire the rich color that shines from it. It's colorful but neutral as well. As I hold it up, a Post-It note falls off. I bend down and pick it up off of the floor.

"I know you can use this somehow. I love you so much Sadie. Love, Auntie Kara"

I remember now. My aunt gave this to me for my eleventh birthday last year. Oh, it's so perfect. As it fills me with inspiration, I hop into my sewing chair and make the most beautiful bodice ever. I pull it out of my machine and hold it up to admire. As it gleams in the light, I feel a sudden rush of joy and happiness. I go through my bin of fabrics again and look at things with a whole new point of view. The sequin fabric can be used beautifully as a trim for the bodice and the skirt for the dress. Next, I find my lace fabric and sew it to the top of the bodice so it drapes over the rest of the soon-to-be dress. I use the linen for the skirt part of the dress so it keeps me cool when I wear the dress. I haven't worn a dress since that horrible first day of second grade, so it kind of has to be light weight and easy-to-wear for me. I put more lace over the linen so it looks fancy like the bodice. I then sew on the sequin fabric as the trim for my dress. It helps hold everything together and gives the dress a nice look to it. I hold up the finished product in the light…light? I look at the time: 3:00AM. Oh gosh. I have to get homework done and then I have to get ready for bed and then I have to-

"Sadie, what are you still doing up?" Mark walks into my room, yawning.

"I was sewing this dress?" It sounds like a question. Ugh. Mark pauses. I look at the dress again, now knowing the time and my situation. It's ugly.

"We have to show Mom. That's amazing." he says.

"Really?" As I look at it again, the inspiration floods back through me. I give him the biggest grin and he gives me one back. We run downstairs to get Mom. But as we get to the stairs, our grins disappear.

"Honey. Are you even listening? I have no choice." Paul says.

"You can't. You just CAN'T. Do you know how that will affect our lives? Do you know that I don't just love you, but my family actually *needs* you! It's not OK to do this. For goodness's sake, I haven't even told the kids yet that we're getting married in October!" Mom argues. *What?* Mark and I walk downstairs slowly and watch from the stairs, trying to not hear anymore secrets tonight. When Mom sees us approach, her face softens. "Hey there kids. What are you guys still doing up? Oh, and Sadie, what is that dress?"

"Well, I've been sewing it and wanted to come down and show you?" *Why does everything I say sound like a question.*

"Oh, it's beautiful." Mom takes it from my arms and twirls it around. "Did you guys finish your homework?"

"Just finished mine." Mark says.

"And you Sadie?"

"Mark's helping me work on it."

"Alright. You two need to get back to your work so you can go to bed. Where's Peter?"

"He's been asleep." Mark and I both say.

"Alright. Love you guys."

"Love you, Mom. Goodnight, Paul." Mark and I both say.

"Goodnight, kids." They say back then glare at each other.

As we run back upstairs, I sit down by my desk and Mark helps me move my sewing machine off of my desk. Then, he pulls up a chair and helps me through my first-day homework. It's always better to be done late than never, a lesson I learned the hard way.

I wake up with a jolt the next morning. I only got a total of two hours of sleep. Mark and I were working from three to four and I have to wake up at six. Ugh. I pull on my dull uniform, brush my hair, and go downstairs for breakfast.

I eat slowly before I fall asleep in my cereal bowl. I wake up a few minutes later with my head in the bowl. Mark and Peter come downstairs soon after I wake up from my nap in the cereal bowl. Mark and I look identical with the sleep in our eyes and the way our body's look worn out. Peter, on the other hand, looks like he's on cloud nine and ready for anything. As they sit down for breakfast, Paul storms out the door without saying a word. Mom runs out of the kitchen, coming after him, knowing that the door slam was him and not a grumpy, sleep deprived teenager. She sticks her bed head out the door and starts cursing at Paul. Then, I hear his car turn on and storm away. Mom brings her head back inside, smooths her hair down, and comes to sit down on one of the two remaining chairs at the table. She kicks the other one across the room. I go back to eating my cereal.

"I'm sorry kids." she says, I look at Mark and Peter. "Things have been happening with Paul and I. I'm not sure I can keep going with him anymore." I literally almost spit out the bite of cereal I just ate.

"You mean you're breaking up with Paul?" I say without even thinking. Mom's eyes start to get watery.

"I believe so. He's found someone else he loves more than me."

Was that the last time I would ever see Paul, let alone Mom somewhat happy? Would we be able to keep our house with Paul gone? Mom comes over and gives us all a group hug. I gulp down my cereal as memories of the last time I saw Dad come flooding back. My eyes start shaking as I hold back tears. What if Paul *never* comes back?

The bus pulls up to the door so I slide on my uniform shoes, grab my backpack, and run out the door. All I want to do right now is stay at home with my mom and brothers where we can all comfort each other. But just like that? Paul is gone? My house? Mom's happiness? I slump onto the bus, thinking about how Mom's life would change. How *my* life would change. I walk to the back of the bus with Marie and Addy and sit quietly in my own thoughts. He just walked away like that? Without a word? What about Peter and Mark? What about me? What about *our lives* he just ruined? I hear Addy and Marie trying to get my attention but I doze off, unable to think about anything other than my family. My family, that was once together years ago, happy. Then Paul I thought for sure was our second chance at maybe a little bit of happiness and he left too. Life will never be the same, and I'm not ready for it to change. One night we were all together and the next morning Dad disappears? One night Mom and Paul were making out on the couch and the next day he disappears too? I'll never be ready. But the only thing I can do, is to not cry in front of everyone. I press my face against the window and look at my house. Through the window I see mom with Mark and Peter, still huddled in that same position. I now regret getting on the bus. I didn't even say bye to them. Do they think I'll run away too? The only thing I can do right is not exactly accept the changes life brings, but to be ready for anything that comes my way.

Chapter 4

 Addy has to shake me violently to get me to wake up when the bus arrives at the school. After I finally wake up, Addy, Marie and I walk down the sidewalk to the entrance of the school. We check our schedules, just in case, to make sure we know what classes to go to.
As we head to our separate classes, I feel a tug on my hair. "Ouch." I say to no one in particular. Then, I hear laughing from behind me. I turn to see Brianna and her posse behind me.
"Nice hair. What salon did you go to? The Bed Head?" All three of them laugh hysterically. I start to argue about how I brushed my hair when I realize that would just make them keep picking on me. I turn back to face forwards. They follow me all the way to math class. I finally turn around.
"You guys aren't even in this class." I say,
"Are we? It just happens to be that my daddy made some arrangements so I could be in every single class with my new bestie."
She comes up to me and puts a piece of chewed gum in my hair. "See ya, bestie." She yells, already halfway down the hall.
Every class? Two was bad enough. I slump down and pull at the gum in my hair. By the time I got to class, I was not able to accomplish getting the gum unstuck but I was able to hide the gum in a hair knot. Blech.

The class went by just like yesterday. Brianna just complaining about everything, me getting through the math problems in a breeze, and the occasional throw of a paper ball. PE went just the same too. The same boy had to climb the rope and Brianna was able to sit out due to a 'twisted ankle'. Mom and Dad and Paul were still on my mind and now Brianna. I was just about ready to bail at that point. When it was my turn to climb the rope, I got about three feet up and fell to the floor. There was a weight on my shoulders I just couldn't lift until I knew more about what was happening with my family. I lay there on the floor of the gym.

"Get up. Stop making a scene." Mrs. Carmelo yells at me. At that last part, "Stop making a scene." I could hear Brianna's heels click against the floor. Then she fell beside me.

"Oh dear, dear, Sadie. I have a twisted ankle and now you. Oh, my bestie. My life will now end." She exclaims. "Let me help you up." She puts my arm over her shoulder and 'tries' to stand up. When she finally does, she collapses on the gym floor, bringing me with down with her.

"Oh dear." Mrs. Carmelo sighs.

I stand up reluctantly and wait in line for the next exercise while Mrs. Carmelo helps Brianna up to the bench.

At lunch, Addy and Marie come sit with me. Then Brianna and her posse. "Oh bestie. How's your ankle?" She exclaims as she sets down her gourmet food from what I assumed was from home.

"Fine." I mumble.

"Oh great. Now that you can walk, we can have a sleepover at my place. What's your phone number, BFF?"

"I have to go to the bathroom." I say as dully as my uniform.

I go into a stall, close the toilet seat and start crying. Not just crying, bawling. I think about the times when Dad and I were younger. I would always try to keep up with my big brothers and always couldn't. Dad would come lift me up and take me across the backyard. I could just imagine the feeling that I was flying. Now I can remember the smell of the freshly mowed lawn and the beautifully pruned flowers not too far away. I could remember later in the night my whole family would sit around the outdoor fireplace, roasting smores at sunset. Then Mom and Dad would always joke, "Look away." And they would exchange a kiss. I would always bury myself in Mark's shirt while he and Peter went "Ewwwww." We were all so happy. All together. And today might have been the last day I ever saw Mom's happiness. With all the pressure of work and now Paul leaving, there's nothing my mom could do. My last glimpse of Paul was just like my last glimpse of Dad: Dashing out the door paying no mind to anyone.

What I would give to be little again. Not again, forever. As I got older, I could keep up with my big brothers not needing Dad's help. Dad would run alongside us while Mom would be in her garden warning us to not go into her vegetables. Why did I rush being little only to get older? I cry harder and harder as the memories blow back into my mind. Eventually I hear the school bell ring cueing the end of lunch. I pay no mind to it as the memories keep coming into my mind. Addy and Marie come running into the bathroom, "Sadie? It's us." Marie's soft voice rings out.

"Yeah. Class starts in a minute. What's wrong?" in Addy's loud booming voice.

"Go away. Both of you. Everyone." I cry back.

"What's wrong, Sadie?" Marie says.

"I'm…fine…" I say.

"No. You're not." Marie says. "You're coming out now, no matter what. I'm going to count to five and I need you to breathe. Then walk out."

"Noooo." I cry.

"1…2…3…4…5."

I try to breathe and slowly unlock the door. They come rushing into the squeezed bathroom stall.

"Oh no. Sadie, are you ok?"

"For the millionth time, what's wrong?" Addy says.

"I can't. I'm staying here till pickup. Something's happened."

"Wh-" I cut Marie off mid-word.

"I'm not ready to talk." I say. Addy pulls me off the seat and Marie helps pull out the gum in my hair. Then they both tug me out of the bathroom and once again, I land straight into Matthew's chest.

"Whoa." he says, "Oh, hi, Sadie."

"Hi." I groan.

"What's wr-"

"Don't ask." Addy says.

"By the way, I'm Marie and this is Addy and I think you know Sadie."

"Hi. I'm Matthew. Nice to meet you." Matthew holds out his hand for them to shake. As Marie and Addy let go of me, I fall to the floor.

"Whoa." Matthew pulls me up. "You good?"

"Yeah." I say, I start to use my muscles again, only to get me to history class.

"I've got her from here." Matthew says. "We're in the same class."

"How should I trus-" Addy starts, holding up a tight fist.

"Thank you." Marie interrupts and pulls Addy's fist down.

Matthew grabs my hand to guide me to class but I feel he has other intentions. I hold on tighter and look back at Addy and Marie. Marie claps excitedly and Addy looks like she's about to punch Matthew's guts out. I look up at Matthew and our eyes meet. I get a little tingle in my stomach when he looks at me. That small feeling gives me enough hope to drag me to class.

When we get to class, the teacher looks at us. "You two again?" She says.

"We're here. Just let us sit down." I say. Definitely not ready for more things to deal with. I might also be feeling more confident in Matthew's arms. That dang stomach tingle.

"This is your first year at this school, I get it, but you two have had tours and everything. Honestly, Brianna knows this school better than you two and this is her second day here. Not a single tour in her past." The teacher says. Brianna smiles and waves like she's won the Olympic gold medal or something. Matthew tries to drop my hand but I hold on tight as we go to take our seats. I raise up straight and stand tall. I have a plan on how to get through my situation. Starting with step one: Get through the day. Other than a few stares in class, everything goes fine. Brianna does nothing, for once. As the class comes to an end Matthew stops me by the doorway and grabs my hands in his. He looks me in the eye and says "I know somethings up. I also know I just met you yesterday. But, do you want to talk about it?"

"It's a long story."

"That's fine."

"No. A really, really, long story." I say back.

"I have time. After school at 4:00?"

"How about ice cream?" I say, starting to brighten up.
Stupid, stupid, stomach tingle.
"It's a date." he says, Then we both blush.
The rest of the day goes by fairly easily except for a few
meltdowns from my new 'bestie.' When the day is over,
my mom doesn't drive to pick me up but Mark. I hop in
the car. "Where's Mom?" "
"She's not doing well."
"Oh." Nothing I didn't expect, I guess. "Anyway, can
you drive me to Ice with the Cream at four 'o' clock?
Please?"
"Why?"
"Just meeting a friend." I say as casually as I can. "It's
good to talk about it sometimes."
"Okay first of all, when have you ever not ended a
sentence sounding like a question?" Peter pops his head
to look at me from behind the passenger seat.
"Um." I start to stress out. I really don't want to spill the
beans. Mark would not approve of me meeting a boy,
alone, being the sensible person that he is.
"I'm messing with you." Peter says. "Sure, Mark can
drive you there. I'll take your shift, brother."
"Right." I say. We drive home talking about our day and
everything that happened. Then Peter brings up the whole
Mom and Paul thing. Mark says nothing. "I'm just not
ready for things to change." I say. Then we drop the
subject and the rest of the ride home is silent

Chapter 5

Mom is in her garden pruning the plants like crazy. I walk outside and stand there watching her for a minute, imagining the little plants as her babies that she's trying to rescue from the real danger, reality.

"Hi." I say, it seems to startle Mom like she just saw a tomato bug on her freshest, juiciest, tomatoes.

"Hello sweetie. How was school?"

"Good. I say. "How's your day?"

"Fun. Just fun." She says sarcastically. "I've been scheduling job interviews for myself but then the bills come in through the mail and I can't seem to get a job quick enough to pay all the bills. Mark and Peter's jobs are helping but-"

I smile at her.

"Sorry sweetie. I can't make sense of anything. Paul and I have been arguing about everything lately and now that I feel he's not coming back anytime soon, I have to take matters into my own hands which seems a lot easier than it actually is."

"I see. By the way, Mark is giving me a ride to Ice with the Cream at four to meet a friend. I didn't know you needed help holding the fort here."

"Oh no sweetie. You go have fun with your friend. You need a break from… from…life." She makes an effort for a smile and I walk upstairs to my room. I get out of my dull uniform and try on my lace dress. It feels like a warm hug that helps me escape from the world. It reminds me of when I was little. Twirling around in my make-believe castle, high in the mountains, waiting for a handsome prince to save me.

"Mark. Peter. Come look." I yell down the hall.

Mark comes in first with Peter slowly trailing behind him. I give them a twirl. "It fits perfectly." I say,
"When did you get this?" Peter asks
"Me? Oh. I sewed this last night."
"Isn't it great?" Mark says. "I usually don't have a good sense of fashion but I knew this was beautiful from the moment I saw it." He smiles.
I give them another twirl. Mark and Peter both start clapping immediately. "I would take that off so it doesn't rip." Mom comes in.
"Good idea." I say, they all exit my room while I change into some casual clothing, my favorite M-TV shirt and some black, ripped, jean shorts. I open the door and go downstairs. I pull on my Converse high tops to match with the rest of my outfit. Since I got out of school at three, I have some time before I have to go to Ice with the Cream so I start working on some homework I didn't get done last night.
"Sadie time to get going." Mark calls. I run outside and jump in the car with Mark. "So, who are you meeting?"
"Um…" Why do I not feel like telling him about Matthew? Seriously, stomach tingle? "Just a friend."
"Ok." Mark says knowingly.
I think he gets what I'm not trying to tell. Since Ice with the Cream is just around the corner, we don't have much time so I hop out of the car, thank Mark for the ride, and head inside to wait for Matthew. I pull out my phone and see my mom texted me.
Let me know when you get there. Love you.
I text her back, letting her know that I'm here safe. Just as I turn my phone off, Matthew walks in the door.
"Hey." I wave at him from the table I sat down in. He waves back and joins me at the seat across the table.
"How are you?" He asks politely.
"Doing better." I say, then laugh.

"Did you already order?" He asks.

"No. I was waiting for you. Do you want to get something?"

"Sure. Ice cream is one of my favorites." He says, then we both laugh. We walk up to the counter and order. I get chocolate drizzled in caramel and Matthew gets mint chocolate chip with a few strawberries as a topping. When we sit down my phone buzzes again.

"Sorry." I say, I look at my phone. Marie texted Addy and I in a group chat asking if we could all get together and talk. At once, I feel bad for not including them in hanging out. I reply quickly, *Sorry. I'm busy. You two go without me. Please. Can we go tomorrow as a group?* Marie responds immediately, *Oh bummer. We won't go without you.*

Then Addy dings in, *Marie and I could go today and do the homework study group?* Addy knows that I hate study groups.

Sure. I wouldn't mind. I reply. *Bye.*

Bye.

See ya.

Before I turn off my phone, I hand it to Matthew. "Can I have your number?" Matthew types it into my phone and hands it back to me. I turn off my phone and look up at Matthew, already half way into his ice cream. "That was Marie and Addy. They were just trying to plan something." I tell him.

"Today? Sorry if I got into your schedule."

"Oh no. It's fine. They're doing a homework study group and I already did mine." He looks at me. "Honestly, I'd rather be here with you than doing homework." I spill. *Whoops.* He laughs. "Really. Thanks for inviting me here, Matthew."

"It was no problem. I just noticed that you weren't like yourself and you needed someone to talk to. I know your friends are super trustworthy, but I can tell you needed someone else. Also, you don't need to call me Matthew. My family calls me Thew." he says.

"Aww. That's a cute nickname. My brothers call me Sade."

"That's cute too. So, to get down to business, what's going on?"

"Well, it's a lot to explain. I still haven't told anyone yet."

"It's fine. It helps if you tell someone how you're feeling rather than keeping it bottled up inside you."

"Who told you that?"

"My mother."

All of a sudden, I feel comfortable to talk to him. "My mom's boyfriend ran away earlier. Just like my dad. Both of them left and drove away to never be seen again. They both left my mom, my two brothers and I with nothing but the house we have to pay for. After Dad ran away, Mom was having a hard time with the house but then Paul came and was able to pay for most of it but with him gone now, I don't know what to expect." And I told him the whole story. Bit by bit. Piece by piece. I cried while explaining the detail of my memories. When I finally stopped talking, coming to the end of the story, I looked up, and his eyes told me something I could never explain in words. Something telling me he was in a deeper situation, but somehow, the same as mine.

"I understand how you feel Sadie. My mom died last
year. We had to pay for a house we had no money for.
My mom was also the one that worked for the family.
When my dad couldn't afford our home anymore, we
moved here. If I'm telling you everything, we now have
to rent a room at the Flowerblush Motel. It's just me and
my dad now."

By the way he emphasized *Mom,* I could tell he was
trying to hold back tears. She must have meant the world
to him.

"Sadie, you remind me of my mother. That's why I felt
so immediately attached to you when you ran into me.
My mother was always running into things in the kitchen
and in the house and actually, my mom claims that's how
she met my dad. I feel such a connection with you
through that."

"I'm so sorry." I say,

"It's not your fault. There was nothing anyone could do
to stop it."

"Yeah." I say helplessly. Then, the door opens wide and
in steps Addy and Marie. "Hey…" I say unsteadily. They
turn their heads to face Thew and I and their faces
change. They look at me in disgust and walk back out the
door. *What's their problem? I can't hang out with anyone
else but them?*

Thew looks at me and asks, "Are they ok?"

"They're fine. They'll get over it." I say, unsure of my
own words. What did I do? "Hey, I really enjoyed talking
to you."

"Maybe next time it can be not *too* depressing." He jokes.
We both get out of our seats, throw our ice creams away,
and head outside. "I'm really sorry about your mom and
dad."

"It's fine. Like you said, there's nothing anyone could
have done to stop it."

"Yeah. Well, it was nice to get to know you." Thew says.
"Yeah, you too. Sorry to cut it short." I say. As soon as he leaves, getting into a very beat down car with his dad, I run in the direction of Addy and Marie. "Addy? Marie?" I call. They couldn't have gotten far. I pull out my phone and call the group chat, while still calling their names. When no one picks up, I can tell they're real angry at me, but for what? What? I start running faster and faster while calling their names louder and louder. What did I do? Finally, I find them sitting in a patch of grass doing homework. As I approach them, Addy gets up.

"What's wrong with you?" She says loud and clear so everyone in the park can hear.

"What?" I say. "What did I do?"

"Hmmm. Hmmmm. What *did* you do exactly? Well, to start, you tell us you're not ready to talk about whatever happened and then, we run into you at Ice with the Cream talking to some dude you met yesterday. That's our place to chill and now you bringing it into *his* life. Then, Brianna comes strolling out of the clothes store just across from Ice with the Cream bragging to us about how you're her new BFF and showed us the matching tutu she bought you and her."

"What? Who said anything about her? I don't even like talking to her. And Matthew, how could you already be so angry at him. All that you've said to him is 'don't ask.' How do you know what he's like?" I yell.

"You don't like talking to Brianna. Really? So, you like hanging out with her and wearing matching tutus, but just not talking to her. That's real nice Sadie." Addy exclaims. "By the way, how do you know Matthew that well. You met him yesterday. Yesterday."

"Ok fine. I hate Brianna."

"Absolutely HATE her?"

"Fine. Yes. I absolutely HATE her.'"
"And what do you say about Matthew?"
I stand their quietly.
"I said, what do you say about Matthew?"
"Nothing. He's fine so far and that's all that matters.
Can't we all be friends?" I say loudly. What's Addy's
problem? "I can hang out with whoever I want. I'm not
saying I hang out with Brianna or even like hanging out
with her, but even if I did, my two best friends should
accept that. Right?"
"What about us? Did you remember *us*? Let us know you
were going out with *him*?" Addy explodes.
"I did. I'll always be there for you guys and remember
you guys. Remember, best friends till the end?"
"Not now." Addy snaps.
"I've had enough to deal with over the last few days and I
don't want anything else on my shoulders to deal with." I
say angrily.
"What has been going on?" Marie peeps in with her soft
but slightly fierce tone.
"Just like my mom and dad did years ago, my mom is
breaking up with stupid Paul who she was apparently
engaged to without me even knowing. There you go?
You happy?" I say.
"Oh no." Marie says. She jumps up to give me a hug but
Addy stops her.
"That's all you had to say. You could have let us known
earlier and everything would have been fine." Addy says.
"That's how you respond. That's how you respond to *my
life*? I wasn't even on a date with him. He's just my
friend." I start screaming now.

"I get it now." I continue. "You're jealous. You're jealous of me hanging out with Matthew. You want to hang out with Brianna because she's the popular girl. You think I'm ditching you guys when really, I just need some comfort from other people. I know you guys will always be at my aide so it's good to have someone else to talk to. And also, I don't even talk to Brianna. *So, stop being jealous.*"

Addy cringes at that last part. "Fine. Go if you want. Go be with your other friends." She sounds hurt now. She starts walking away.

"Addy, wait." Now I feel bad. "I didn't mean to hurt your feelings."

"Well, you did." She cries. I start running after her but Marie puts a hand on my shoulder.

"Don't." She says softly. Then she walks away too. I fall on the grass beneath me and cry. I cry into the Earth, waiting for it to consume me and let me know I don't belong anywhere. Not here, not there, not anywhere. I'm alone in this world and I have to face it. No one can tell me otherwise because it's the truth. I pull out my phone and dial Marks number. He picks up right away.

"Hello?"

"I'm ready to be picked up." I cry softly.

"What happened?" He asks urgently.

"I'll tell you on the way." I cry harder.

"Be there in a jiffy." You can hear the car engine turn on in the background and he hangs up. I put my phone back in my pocket and lay face first in the grass. I don't care who sees me or what they think of me. I'm staying right here and I'm not moving until Mark comes and takes me to where I can lock myself in my room and never come out.

Chapter 6

When Mark's red Toyota Corolla pulls up, he hops out of the car and runs straight to where I'm lying in the grass. "What happened?" He asks.

"It's Addy and Marie." I cry. Since he's super tall and super muscular, he bends down and lifts me up off the ground. He cradles me in his arms like a baby and carries me to the car. He sets me in the backseat so I can lay down.

When we get on the road, I tell him all about everything that happened. I tell him about how I never told anyone about Thew and how Marie and Addy got so angry when they walked in and saw us. I told him about how they wouldn't answer my calls and the huge argument I had with Addy.

When I finish, all he says is "Wow." Being the sensible person that he is, I expect he would never get into a pickle like this. "I'm really sorry. Honestly, I don't know what to tell you."

"I know. I couldn't expect you to handle that."

"No. No. I'm glad that you told me."

"Mhm." I reply.

"How about we go to Amelia's?"

"Really?" My mood brightens a little bit.

"Sure thing. You've had a rough day. I'll give you twenty dollars to spend. Got it? Only twenty. Not a cent more."

"Thank you so much!"

We pull into the parking lot and Mark gives me a twenty dollar bill out of his wallet. "Want me to come in with you or do you want me stay in the car?"

"I've got it. Unless, you want to come?" I raise my eyebrows.

"Sure." He takes out the key and puts it in his pocket. I get out of the car and walk up to the sidewalk to stand under the awning of my favorite store ever, Amelia's. I walk through the automatic doors with Mark following a ways behind me. As soon as I walk into the store, the smell of fresh fabrics and newly made sewing machines makes me bounce with excitement.

"You sure you've got it?" Mark asks.

"Yes, obviously." I reply. Mark and I have had this tradition ever since I started sewing when I was eight. He would take me here and give me the same rules: "Twenty dollars. Not a cent more." He would wait by the entrance and talk to an old friend of his that he went to intermediate school with. She works as a cashier. As soon as he walks over to the side of the counter that her register is at, I run off into the first aisle of fabrics. These are the older fabrics that are on clearance, one of my favorite aisles for obvious reasons. Cheaper material equals more things that I can buy. I find a pretty baby blue fabric and a few swatches of a rosy pink one too. After I've gone down that aisle about six or seven times, I move onto the next aisle where the fabrics that are *about* to be on clearance are displayed. I've been to this store so many times, I don't bother going down this aisle more than once knowing that in about three days, they'll recycle the clearance fabrics and replace them with these ones at a much cheaper price than they are now. I move onto the next aisle and find a few sequin ones that I like but decide no on, only because of my budget. I keep going down the aisles one by one until I reach the last aisle with the newest fabrics. I start to head down the aisle when I see Brianna and her father. I freeze and start backing up slowly until I'm hidden behind a wall display between that aisle and the one before it. I peek my head around to see what they're doing.

"I said I wanted *that* gold one, not the one that you're holding. The one that you're holding is not *real* silk!"
"Madame, this one's a lot cheaper than the one you want." Her father says. But wait. It's not her father. It's her *butler*. I shriek at the realization and cover my mouth immediately. Thank goodness she doesn't hear.
"I just told you that I didn't want that one. Are you arguing with me? I can just tell Daddy that you're not doing what I want and he'll fire you and your ugly wife sooner than you can say 'madame.'"
"No, madame. There is no need to call your father. I was just-"
"But, but, but! One more word and you'll be fired."
"Of course." The butler sets down the gold fabric he's holding and grabs the one Brianna wants.
"You know what? I actually don't like the food your wife cooks and you've been arguing with me a lot more recently. I've made up my mind." Brianna pulls out her phone with a sparkly pink case and dials someone's phone number. "Daddy! I order you to fire my butler and my chef! They are both mean and argumentative and I can't deal with it anymore!" She pauses to hear her father's response. "Actually, while you're at it, my maid didn't clean my mirror for me last night when I asked her to. She told me she'd just cleaned it so fire her too." She pauses again and hangs up the phone.
After about five minutes with the butler apologizing to Brianna and begging for her forgiveness, a bigger, stronger, man wearing a neater black suit and tie walks up and holds Brianna's *real silk* gold fabric. The new butler whispers something into the first butler's ear. Butler One's shoulders sag as he walks out of the store, dramatically throwing his pearly white gloves on to the floor.

"Hmph." Brianna glares at the gloves he left on the floor. "I order you to pick those up. Now."

"Of course, ma'am."

"Madame." She corrects. Butler Two starts walking up to where Butler One's gloves lay, right in front of my feet. I turn quickly and start jogging into the next aisle, dragging all my fabrics with me. I see the butler and Brianna walk up to the cashier with the whole role of pure gold silk fabric. Whenever they walk out of the store, I immediately relax and head over to the aisle that they were in. I find only one fabric that I like and head over to the back of the store where I can shop for patterns, bobbins, and thread. I find only a small case of bobbins that I need for my machine and head to the cashier.

"Hey Sadie, how've you been?" Mark's friend and cashier, Rebecca, asks me, her blue eyes gleaming.

"Fine, I guess. How about you?"

"I've actually been pretty good." She smiles. "I was telling your brother Mark this earlier but I got, well, more than a promotion I guess." She smiles wider. "Amelia is retiring and out of all the workers here, she chose me to take over the whole entire store."

"Really? That's crazy. Congratulations."

"Thanks." She tucks her wavy blonde hair behind her ear. "Mark already promised he'd take you here a lot more than usual since I'll be in charge."

"Does that mean we get a discount?"

"Well, if you really insist," Rebecca grins. I grin back at Rebecca and she hands me my bag of cloth and bobbins. "I took off a little today as well. Just the usual, twenty dollars and not cent more."

Mark smiles and we wave goodbye and hop in the car.

When we arrive home, I run straight to my room and lock myself inside with my new fabrics. I pull out my sewing machine and put the new dress I sewed on a mannequin for inspiration. I pull out some more of the lace I used last night and the leftover silk my aunt gave me. There was only a tiny bit of the silk left so I just sew a little bow with the lace in the middle to go in my hair as a hair tie. I pin it to the mannequin's head to give me a good visual of my outfit. I stand there, admiring my creation and imagining what I can do with the new fabrics I just got today until I hear a knock on my door. "Who is it?" I call.
"It's your mother, mind you." She says jokingly. I come to the door and let her in. "Mark told me what happened. I'm really, truly, sorry for you. Friends have arguments sometimes,"
"It was a fight. Not an argument." I correct her, my bad mood returning.
"Excuse me. Friends have *fights* sometimes and that's just part of life. Personally, I think the three of you will get back together. The three of you have been friends since you met in preschool. Friends like that don't come around every day."
"I know Mom. It's just that, why can't I hang out with other people other than them?" I ask her.
"Sweetie, you can. It's just that the three of you have been friends for a long time so it's hard for your friends to see you with someone else. Especially with a boy."
She winks at me.
"Mo-om." I say. "Mark wasn't supposed to tell you about that."
"So, tell me about this Matthew boy. Is he cute?"
I laugh. "Did Mark *really* have to tell you this?"
Mom smiles.

"Yes." I admit, answering her question. "It's his eyes the most though. They have this, magical sparkle in them that you find hard to look away from."
"I see." Mom says knowingly.
"Although really, he's super nice and he already knows me super well. He could tell I wasn't doing very well when I walked straight into him."
"Those are the best type." Mom says, then giggles. Her laughter causes a chain reaction and I start laughing too.
 Mark comes in "You feeling better? What's going on?" Then he starts laughing too at the ridiculous situation before him. A twelve-year-old after a huge fight with her friends and a Mom who just broke up with her fiancé laughing hysterically on the ground.
Peter runs in "Why is it so loud in here?" Then he sees us all sitting on the floor laughing our heads off and comes and joins us. "What's so funny?" He laughs.
"This boy in school, I can't tell you how many times I've run into him. Splat into the chest." Then enormous laughter. "Seriously. He's always right there." I giggle. Then the room sounds like a pack of wild hyenas. I don't think what I said was so funny, but the fact that we're all laughing considering what happened earlier, I'll keep it up. We laughed for probably two hours until Mom finally said it was time for bed. I crawl into bed and grab the diary I've never even written in.

Dear diary,

I think I have a crush.

The next few weeks go by in a blur. Same old, same old. At school, Brianna still shows up late to class everyday with some stupid princess excuse, Addy and Marie keep ignoring me, and I've been sitting with Thew and some of his friends at lunch. After school, I get home, do my homework, sew for a bit, and every Wednesday, I meet up with Thew at Ice with the Cream. After I get home, at 6:30, we have an hour officially marked as laughing hour when we just laugh about the day and at life. For some reason, every little thing just seems like the funniest joke you've heard in your life. There're new ones every day too. It turns out, since Paul left, life has been a bit happier. Mom still misses him, of course, but she's so much happier, it's contagious and weird at the same time.

Even though school started and Mom broke up in August, things have been so much better and it's only mid-September. Mark and Peter and I were already gathered around my room, ready for laughing hour, and waiting for Mom.
"When is she going to be here?" Peter asks.
Right on cue, Mom comes in. "Hi, guys. Sorry I'm late. I have some bad news." We all look up at her. "I can only afford a few more days in this house. The bills and taxes came in the mail today and it's too much to afford."
"What?" Mark, Peter, and I all yell simultaneously.
"Yes. Yes. I know. All three of you grew up here. This is the house I bought with your father. This was the house…" She trails off. Then a single tear slides down her face.

Most times it's a blessing that Mom's mood is contagious but now is not one of the good times. A tear slides down my face and Peter and Mark each put one arm around me. Mom plops down on the floor with us and we all hug each other tightly. Then, everything is silent. All there is is the small whimpering of a hurt dog that is called my heart.

The next morning, I walk downstairs into the lake of boxes. Mom must've been up all night to have the living room packed up already. I go to school without any breakfast, having lost my appetite last night before dinner. I hop on the bus and stay towards the front of the bus, my new bus seat with Thew. When I sit down, I look him in the eye and say quietly, "We're moving."

"What?" He yells a little too loudly.

"Yeah. My mom told us last night. I don't even know where we're going."

"Did you start packing already?" Thew sounds panicked.

"Yes." I whisper. I lean into his chest and start crying. The good part about Thew is that ever since I really got to know him, I've been able to rely on him better than anyone else. As the bus starts moving, I don't move with it. I feel the stares on the back of my head from probably everybody on the bus. When Thew and I get to school, I reluctantly get up, still in his arms. He walks me all the way to my first class and the leaves me at the door.

"Your goal is to get through the day." He tells me.

"My goal, is to get through the day." I repeat. I slowly walk into the class, take my seat, and try to focus on the lesson while my mind drifts elsewhere. That's how it is through the whole day until lunch, when I go sit with Addy and Marie at our old table. "I'm moving." I say quietly. You can tell Addy tries to look all calm and cool but her voice sounds different when she talks. Not angry, but sad.

"Good." She quivers.

"I know you guys are still really angry at me and I'm sorry for that. I just…I guess I wanted to tell my best friends that I'm leaving." I say. Marie runs up and gives me a hug and Addy doesn't stop her. School goes by like every other day and the end of the day comes in no time. Thank goodness.

After school, I meet up with Thew at the bus stop. "Do you want to go get ice cream with me after school?" I ask him sadly. "It might be our last."

"Don't think like that, Sade. Of course, I'll go with you after school. Same time as usual?"

"Sure." I say, When the bus gets to the stop, I hop on with Thew and his friends and I take the bus home. His friends try to do funny stuff to make me laugh but nothing works. At my stop, I hop off and wave at everyone on the bus.

As soon as I get inside the house, I notice that the lake of boxes has turned into a river. All of the neighbors were inside the house packing everything that we own. Mom pokes her head out from behind one of the box walls.

"Welcome home sweetie. Some neighbors heard about what happened and then word got out and now the whole neighborhood is helping out." She yells over the vacuum cleaner. I make an effort for a smile. "Don't worry. We left your room just the same." Mom adds.

I walk upstairs to my room and see that as a matter of fact, nothing was touched. I take off my uniform and put on some normal clothes. Then I grab some boxes that were laid carefully outside my room and start packing my things. I gather my clothes and put them in one box, well two, and put my glass collectables Dad always got me in another. I was packing and packing and lost track of time. Before I knew it, it was time to go.

I had Mark drive me to Ice with the Cream, once again, and got out just as the clock struck 4:00. He was already inside waiting at our normal table with his favorite ice cream and my favorite ice cream. When I sit down at the table, he starts with casual talk. How was your day? How's your family? "You can tell I'm trying to sugarcoat this, can't you?"

"Yep." I say.

"Dammit I'm really going to miss you." Thew says. "Do you know where you're moving yet?"

"For some reason, I still don't know."

"So, it was too expensive here?"

"Yes. My mom couldn't find work. So, we are probably heading out of state."

"My dad had that same problem when we first started off." Thew says.

"And he finally found a job and an affordable place?" I ask.

"After a while, yes. You could stay with me. I'd be happy to have you."

"Yeah right. Like my mom would be down with that, let alone my brothers. Besides, you already have hardly enough room to live with just you and your dad."

"I know, I know. I just wish there was a way you could stay here." He says as he looks me in the eye.

We kept talking about how he and his father managed and thought maybe there was a way my family could just downsize to an apartment.

"When the bus pulled up at your house, I saw there were some neighbors helping to pack up. My father and I would love to help. I mean, like, if you don't mind?"

"Of course. It would be great to have a friend there." I say.

"Aren't we just a little bit more than friends at this point?" Thew adds.

I smile. He looks up at me and smiles too. "We can do this." He says.

Chapter 7

When Thew's dad comes to pick the two of us up, Thew and I slide into the backseat.

"It was all Matthew's idea to come help out." Mr. Clint says.

"That's nice that Matthew wants to come." I say and look into his eyes.

"Why do you sound so excited about moving?" Mr. Clint asks.

"I'm not excited about it. I just accept it." I say. "You know, I really, really, don't want to move."

"I think you've mistaken her emotions, Dad." Thew says.

"It's funny because I thought life was finally, how would you say it, ok again, and now I have to move." I say. "I was finally just a tiny bit happy and then, boom. Everything's in boxes. Literally."

Then we arrive back to my home and we get out of the car. I stand with Thew as we walk into the house. "You can come help me with my room." I tell Thew. Then, the door opens and we run upstairs as Thew's dad greets my mother.

"You're almost done packing already." Thew says under his breath.

"I know." I say sadly. I stand on my bed and start taking down old photos that hang on the walls. I'm completely fine until I pause to look at a photo frame with four slots. Mom, Dad, Mark, and Peter all looking at me whenever I was first brought home from the hospital, me eating my very first cupcake when I was three, my sixth-grade graduation photo, and a selfie of Thew and I that we took a few weeks ago. I guess Thew notices me because he takes me out of my deep thoughts. "You, ok?"

"Yes." I start to tear up. In front of Thew. Again. He carries me off of my bed and sits me down in my sewing chair.

"I'm not going to tell you everything's going to be fine." He says, reading my mind.

"I know." I cry. I fall out of my chair on purpose and sit on to the floor right next to where Thew is sitting. He wraps me in an embrace that I never want to get out of. I feel warm and immediately comforted by his arms. I lay my head on his shoulder and an electric spark runs through my body. Nothing is going to ruin this moment, not even that stupid stomach tingle. Most likely one of my last moments with Thew. I hear a slight knock on the door. "Yes." I say feeling a bit better, but still crying.

"It's Mark. May I come in?"

"Yes." Thew answers for me. Mark walks inside and closes the door behind him.

"Sorry if I disturbed something." He says, looking down on Thew and I. "Just wanted to let you know, Sade, that we're leaving for New York in two days. We're staying with Aunt Kara."

"Two days?" Thew and I both gape.

"Sadly, yes. Mom said that it was one of the only flights available. Aunt Kara is paying for everything."

Instead of unwrapping myself from Thew's arms to make eye contact with Mark, I cuddle deeper inside trying to escape from reality.

"You have the option to go to school tomorrow or not. You decide." Mark adds. Then he walks out of the room, knowing he's not getting an answer from me anytime soon.

Thew and I just sit there silently, not talking, not packing boxes, just sitting. We each are thinking our own thoughts but, in some way, I know what he's thinking and he knows what I'm thinking.

"Will you come to the airport with us when it's time to leave?" I whisper.

"Wouldn't miss it for the world." He responds.

I weep in his arms not knowing what to do anymore. My original plan was to go with the flow but how could I just "go with the flow" at this point? Things started looking up for me and now I'm just right back where I started. Except worse. My journey, my life, is pointless. My best friends hate me, my dad's nowhere to be seen, I'm homeless and going to be living with my aunt, and on top of it, far, far away from where I once had a small sense that I belonged.

"Sadie?"

"Yes?"

"I need to tell you something."

"I'm not interrupting." I slow my crying as much as possible.

"I've always been an outcast. Someone who was either looked over or bullied for being the 'weird kid' or 'the kid with no money.' I've felt like those titles have controlled my life until that first day when you bumped into me. Ever since then, my life has been transformed into something amazing. Something that only exists because of you. And I love you for that and for so many other reasons, too much to tell."

"Thew, really? Right now?"

"Sadie, I love you. Even in your worst moments."

"Thew, seventh grade, remember?"

"Sade, I understand, but you've made my life so much better. You can't leave now. I love you, Sadie." Thew starts crying.

Thew's dad and my mom came in to tell us it was time for Thew to go. I wouldn't let Thew get up, so they walked inside the room and looked quite shocked. Well, my mom did. Thew's dad just smiled, like he knew this was happening all along. My mom looked like she was about to yell, but then her face softened and she had that same smile Thew's dad had. I look at Thew in the eyes and I could feel something was about to happen, even though his dad and my mom were right there. He starts to lean in close to my face and I close my eyes. *I'll let it happen. I really will.* I let the stomach tingle take over and…and feel my mom grab my shoulders. I open my eyes and look up at her above me. I give an innocent smile and she gives me the *not-today-young-lady* face. I stand up as Thew's dad takes him out of the room. He looks behind his dad to see me. I mouth "See you at school tomorrow." And he smiles.

I finish packing late at night and fall right asleep in my bed. All night I dream of not moving, or seeing my aunt, but 'the what could've been' my first kiss. I know Mom would have never approved, but I'm in seventh grade now. Is that even old enough for a kiss though? I wasn't angry. I wasn't sad anymore. I was happy. Today wasn't my day, but some day in the very-near-future, I will get that kiss. When we leave in two days, it won't be the last time I'll see him. It'll be the day I say "See you again soon."

Morning comes too soon the next day. Instead of my normal alarm clock, Peter comes marching in with his bongo drum and Mark with Peter's old trumpet.
"It's morning. It's morning. Time to go to schoo-ool. Get up. Get up. Morning already…" Great. The finale.
"Hereeeeeeeeeeeeeeee." Peter sings loudly.

I open my eyes just a little bit to see them. They start singing the song over since I'm not out of bed yet. "It's morning. It's morning." *Ugh.* I get out bed and go to the box with my clothes in it. Peter keeps singing. "Get up. Get up." I grab the school uniform I laid on the top of one of the boxes for easy access. "Morning already…" I take off my sleeping socks. "Hereeeeeeeee-"

"Are you guys going to give me privacy?" I accidentally snap, interrupting Peter's finale. The two walk down the hall into Mom's room and start the song over. You can hear it echo through the empty hall. I pull off the rest of my clothes, take a fast shower, and pull on my uniform. I walk to the mirror and braid my hair, one of my favorite hairstyles. I walk downstairs into the now sea of boxes. Our dining table was already moved and is outside for sale as well as most of our furniture. Our cereal and bowls went somewhere and our fridge was already empty. Since the town was just around the corner, I pull on my backpack, yell upstairs at Mark, Peter, and my mom that I'm going out for breakfast. I walk down the street, past our neighbors' houses and into the little town. I look at some breakfast options and decide on Mason's Cakes. They make delicious cakes for birthdays, anniversaries, graduations, and everything you can think of. They also have world's best pancakes that I've had over a million times. I walk inside to be greeted by one of my old babysitters, Sonata. "Hey, Sadie. You want the usual?" She asks.

"Yes please." I say, already in a better mood. I sit down in one of their antique, pink, table sets. I check the time using my phone. Being on time usually isn't my top priority, but today, I need to make a good last impression. I have exactly twenty-two minutes until the bus stops at my house and since it takes two minutes to get to the town from my house, it should take two minutes to get back. So, I'll leave in exactly twenty minutes. Simple math problem. Marie would be proud. After about five minutes, my favorite breakfast plate is set before me. Two blueberry pancakes, a side of bacon and fruit, and a pink lemonade raspberry smoothie.

"How's life been treat'n ya'll?" Sonata says. She moved from the country a few years back when she was seventeen and my mom hired her as a babysitter since Mark and Peter weren't old enough to take care of me yet.

"Well, I'm moving tomorrow."

Sonata gasps. "How far away?"

"New York."

"Sweet baby boots. The meal's on the house today. We'll miss ya'll around here."

"I'll miss you too. Also, I brought some cash to pay."

"Oh please no. We've got enough money to own twelve farms making not one penny at all."

She didn't have to tell me twice. "Thank you so much, Sonata."

She winks and walks away to serve another customer. I dive in to my food having wasted a minute and a half talking to Sonata.

As I bite into the blueberry pancake, a burst of flavor explodes in my mouth. It tastes sweeter than sugar could ever be. I devour my pancakes and slurp down my smoothie. I pop the grapes from the fruit bowl into my mouth and wipe off my hands from the grease the bacon had left behind. I finish my meal just in time. I wave at Sonata and she waves back. I jog down the street taking in all the scenery I may never see again. I get into my neighborhood and beat the bus by thirty seconds. I walk onto the bus and file into the seat with Thew and his friends. As we ride to school, I tell everyone that this is the last day I'll be seeing them. Brianna does this dramatic fake cry and everyone stares at her. While she has all the attention, I lay my head on Thew's chest and gaze out the window.

When we get to school, everyone hugs me and says their goodbyes. Our schedule was different though. As we file into our classrooms, the teachers lead us right back out. Everyone in the whole entire school comes out into the hallway and goes into the gym, the biggest room on campus. When we walk inside though, it's not our normal gym. It has a huge stage set up with a single microphone in the middle and a bunch of fold out chairs. When we all take our seats, the new principal walks onto the stage to the microphone.

"Welcome. Welcome. As many of you know, my name is Dr. Goldy Bronzeono. People call me Dr. Bronze for short." She pauses for an applause but the only person clapping and cheering is Brianna. "Oh, thank you, thank you everyone. I've gathered you here today for a special announcement." *Is she announcing that I'm leaving?* I think to myself. *Maybe she isn't half bad.* "This year, we have our fall dance. In exactly one month from today, Fall will arrive and we will be dancing the night away."

In the gym, you can hear all the girls laugh with joy and the boys sigh with sadness. "Boys, it's your duty to ask the girls out to the dance. Ladies, try your best to make the gentlemen happy with their decision. All day today, instead of classes, we will be decorating the gym for the dance. We will also have a table open for volunteers. The spots available for sign up are the coordinator and the DJ." Everyone gasps.

"Yes, yes." She continues. "This year we will be having a DJ from our own school. Auditions take place in room 402. Coordinators will gather in room 450. The night of the fall dance, we will also be having an election for school president. Please go to room 503 if you are interested." Everyone cheers. "I thought so. But to make this year more fun, it's an assignment that the boy must ask the girl to dance. Every single gentleman must have a lady to dance with at the party. Thank you so much and enjoy the rest of the day."

Everyone claps and cheers, except for me. In a month, I'll be in New York. Some boy won't have a partner and I think I know who it will be. As everyone gets out of their seats, there's a big huddle over the sign-up sheets for DJ and coordinators. A quarter of the room runs outside to room 503 and the rest of the kids, including me, head over to the decorations closet to get started. The staff who work at the school take the fold up chairs back to the chair closet to make room for the decorations. Thew finds me in the crowd and we both work on hanging balloons around the gym. The balloons are all purple, and teal even though it's a fall party. Strange. After the gym is full of balloons, I climb up the rope to throw streamers over the lights. "Hey, Thew?"

"Yeah? What's up?"

"Me, obviously."

"Ok, ok, smarty. What's *really* up?"

"Just wanted to say sorry about last night. I was kind of a mess." I slide down the super tall rope one last time and land straight on my feet. Finally.

Thew and I begin to tape streamers over the door so when someone enters, they walk through a wall of streamers. Thew and I also help place tiles onto the floor to use as a dance floor. We then added floor lights to the tiles to make a *real* dance floor. Then, a girl in some honors class, was quickly building a remote out of old circuit boards and recycled milk boxes that could control the lights. She made them flash a rainbow of colors and then created a program to make them flash purple and teal to match the balloons. Soon enough, it was a just a few kids who were left decorating because the others went to audition for coordinators, school president, or DJ. Addy and Marie were nowhere to be seen. They were probably auditioning. As I helped the techy girl with her remote, Thew went to go help a group of boys lift the DJ booth up onto the stage.

"You're really good at that stuff." I say pointing to the remote in the girl's hand.

"Thank you. I'm Gerta."

"Sadie." I say holding out my hand. She shakes it.

For a while she helps teach me how to use the remote and then how to program it. After a while of teaching, I finally got it. We sat on the floor making little tweaks to the remote. After a while, we got the lights to dance to the beat. "Sing." she said. I sat there for a second, weighing my options. She nodded expectantly. Well, I'll start off by singing the first thing on my mind:

It's morning. It's morning.

Time to go to schoo-ool.

Get up. Get up.

Morning already… Hereeeeeeeeeeeeeee.

The lights flash to my song. Then soon, Gerta gets the song and starts singing along. The lights are a beautiful show that someone could watch for hours. They'll be perfect for the dance. That I'll never go to. I stand back to admire the whole gym. "Wow." I say under my breath. It doesn't look like a gym at all, it looks like somewhat of a night club. Goal achieved. I walk back even farther to the door. Back, back, back, boom. I crash right into Thew.
"It's not smart to walk backwards." He jokes.
"How many times is that now?" I ask.
"Three." He responds.
"Three? Seriously?"
"Two times outside the bathroom and one time now." He holds up his fingers. Two on one hand one on the other.
"Oh, shut up." I say, laughing. The rest of the day goes by too quickly. At lunch, Marie and Addy join Thew and I at a table. We talk casually and all three of them blab on and on about how they'll miss me. Even Addy. At that, I'm taken by surprise and I'm laughing and crying at the same time.
At the end of the day, we all gather up at the bus stop and I say a super long, heartfelt, goodbye to Marie and Addy and they actually let me hug them. For a long time. When the bus pulls up to my house, Thew gets out with me. We walk inside the house and Thew's dad is helping to get the final boxes packed and loaded onto the truck parked outside. My room is empty. There is not a sign that once humans stayed here. And not just in my room, in the whole house. The only thing left in the house is a few sleeping bags on the floor that is to be my family's beds for the night. Thew holds my hand and I lean into him.
"Nothing's going to be the same."
"Never." he says.

Chapter 8

Last night was a painful sleep. I only closed my eyes for two hours the whole entire night. No dreams either. Only thoughts of the nightmare I'm living. The only good part in my living nightmare is Thew, my friends, and family. Life in New York was just what I wanted a few months ago. I dreamed about staying with my aunt in her huge house and going to a private school with no annoying *Briannas* or anyone to start a fight with. Now, I'm going there. I'm going to my live my childhood dreams. In just two hours, we get on a plane going far away from everything I love. Of course, Mark, Peter, and Mom are coming with me, but Dad is still out there. I still have a small hint of hope that he might return someday. And Addy and Marie, they're my best friends. Somehow, I feel like at lunch yesterday, we made up for any past fights. And not to mention Thew. Well, there's not much to say about him. He's cute, he's nice, and he understands me like no one else does. These kinds of people don't come around every day.

I take one last look at the empty house to make sure I'm not forgetting anything, and walk outside with the rest of my family. I walk outside and Thew's dad's car pulls up to take us to the airport. Thew and I go to the very back, Mark and Peter in the row in front of us, and Mom with Thew's dad in the very front. Mom looks back at Thew and I.

"Now there, no kissing in the backseat."

"We won't Mom." I say, then roll my eyes.

"Teenagers." Mom mumbles.

I lay on Thew's shoulder the whole time and look out the window at everything that I'll miss. Mason's Cakes, Ice with the Cream, my home behind me, even school. I'll miss every last bit of it. Even Brianna. What's school without a girl who thinks she's, what would I call it, the queen of all things. My life will never be the same. At that thought, Thew wraps me in his arms again. "I'll miss you." I feel something wet on my shoulder. I look up at him.

"Are you crying?" I ask.

"No. Just, have something in my eye."

"Of course." I try to joke. We both give each other a weak smile and we both start to have a meltdown. We cry quietly and no one seems to notice. The whole way to the airport, we cry. Mark looks back at us at one point but being my big brother and a sensible person, he lets us cry it out without saying a word. When we get to the airport, all six of us get out and walk to the TSA line where my family and Thew's will be ripped apart forever.

Exactly one hour until we depart. Our bags are all checked and getting loaded onto the plane while Mom talks Mr. Clint's head off about how she thanks him for everything and how he's such a kind gentleman and on and on and on. Mark and Peter ran off already to wait by the gate and order food. That just leaves Thew and I. He grabs my hands in his as our final goodbye starts.

"Sadie, you'll be back in a month, right? You know, to visit?"

"I can't make any promises."

"Well, for the assignment, will you be my date to the fall dance?" There's a small glimmer of hope in his eyes that I've never seen before. It makes them glitter in the light like everything in the world revolves around his eyes.

"Oh, stop it. Of course." I cry.

The mic turns on. "Early boarding for flight 206 to New York City. Please make your way to gate 18 for early boarding to New York City. Thank you."

I run into Thew's arms. I cry the hardest I've ever cried. I love him and I know it. As much as I try to tell myself I'm too young and that it's just a small crush, my doubting words *disappear*. No one can tell me otherwise.

"Thew, I love you." I say quietly.

"Sadie, I love you too." He leans in for a kiss but I put a finger to his lips. He looks surprised as our kiss is interrupted again.

"If you don't kiss me now, it means I owe you one. I'm coming back someday for that kiss. I'll see you again." He grasps my hands tighter. "I trust you."

I give him one last hug and run out of the line where Mom is waiting for me. Hand in hand, Mom and I see the flight attendant come out of the gateway and start scanning tickets. My brothers walk on board and my mom waves at Thew and his dad. Then she walks on. But I stand there, Mom pulling my hand, unable to look away from where I'm leaving. Who I'm leaving. Then, out of nowhere, Addy and Marie run to the TSA line, as close to where I'm standing as they can get.

"It took a lot to convince my dad." Addy says, out of breath. "It also took a lot to convince her to miss school."

Marie smiles. "You're our best friend. Of course, we would come." She says reading the look on my face.

"Safe travels, my friend." Addy says, trying to sound official.

"We'll miss you." Marie says. I jump under the rope of the TSA line and they both come in for a hug. I cry. They squeeze. We're all one big mess.

"Best friends till the end." I cry.

They nod in agreement and start crying too. Then they back up so I can see Thew. He runs in for one last hug too. He rocks me in his arms as we hug and I know I'm going to miss him. All of them. Then, they all back up as more people come to get through TSA.

"I love you." I mouth at Thew.

"I love you too." He mouths back.

I look at Addy and Marie and give them a strong smile that tells them all will be ok. They know exactly what I mean.

I look at Thew's dad and yell "Thank you."

We all wave at each other and I run to join my family on the plane to New York City.

Chapter 9

When the plane takes off, I sit quietly in my seat in between Mark and Peter. They decided I shouldn't have the window seat because I'd start crying again. Mark nudges me.

"It's going to be a long flight if you spend it like that."

I nod and turn on the movie screen that's hooked up to the chair in front of me. All of these movies for free? I scroll through the list of movies and decide on one of my favorites, *The Hunger Games*. I watch the movie all the way through the credits and once it finishes, I turn off my screen and poke Mark.

"Are we there yet?"

He looks down from his screen. "No. Not even close."

"Ugh." I turn back on my screen and find nothing else good to watch. And now I'm stuck on a plane in midair. I pull out my phone and pay for the plane's Wi-Fi. Then, I text Thew.

Me: Did you get back to school safely?

Thew: Yeah. We're just decorating the gym more.

Me: Wish I was there.

Thew: Everyone misses you.

Me: I bet. LOL

Thew: Want to talk to Addy?

Me: Of course.

Thew/Addy: Hey. You at your aunt's?

Me: No. Still on the plane.

Thew/Addy: Have you seen the Walking Dead series?

Me: No. (And I don't plan to)

Thew/Addy: I'm gonna get back to décor. Miss you already.

Me: You too.

Thew: Marie's in with the coordinators now so she's not around to talk.

Me: Good for her. Tell her I said hi.
Thew: Ok. Addy tried out for DJ and the judges are going through auditions and scores today.
*Me: *Crossing fingers**
Thew: Me too.
Me: Well, don't want you to get into trouble. I'll let you go. I promise to call you once I get settled in. Miss you.
Thew: Miss you too. See ya.

I turn off my phone and look through the movies again. With no luck, I turn to Mark. "You know how Aunt Kara keeps those rooms open for us for when we visit?"

Mark pulls his headphones off. "Yeah. What about them?"

"Do you think she's upgraded them since we're, like, technically living with her now?"

"You know, that's a smart thought. But why would she spend so much money on her place instead of just helping us buy a house?"

"Good point." I say. I can tell Mark is also upset about not having a house to call our own. I decide to leave it at that and turn on YouTube to watch my favorite channel, Fashion on the Run. It's kind of cheesy but the clothes people design are pretty awesome. They created a TV show that's coming out next week that I'm pretty excited about. Marie watches the channel too so I was going to have her come over to binge it with me, but I don't think that's going to happen.

I turn on the first video which happens to be a live stream. It's the main girl who started the channel, Ashely, talking about the new show next week. I plug in my ear buds and tune in.

"Hey, hey, hey everyone. Welcome or welcome back to Fashion on the Run. I'm Ashely. I just wanted to come on and let everyone know how excited I am for the new show next week, Fashion on the Run: New York." *Wait. New York? That's where I'm going to be.* "It's a fashion show, of course, but it's really a game. We're taking contestants in from all over the US. Auditions take place in the new studio built especially for my new show. We call it FOTR for Fashion on the Run. Stop by if you think you're great enough to compete on a competition televised all over the US. I posted the address in the comments. Catch you later!"

The broadcast ends but is followed by a commercial for the new show. It takes a minute for my brain to process the information. A fashion show competition. On TV. In New York. That I can possibly audition for.

The commercial interrupts my thoughts. "Thirteen contestants." *(Dramatic music.)* "Competing for one cash prize." *(More dramatic music.)* "By sewing their hearts out." *(Weird smushy mushy music)* "All on one show." *(Exciting music.)* "Tune in Friday at eight 'o'clock for auditions."

Ok. A "cash prize?" Bingo. I send the link of the video to Mark and I see him click it. Meanwhile, I click the link of the address in the comments. Right smack dab in the middle of 53rd Avenue. Then, I scan across the map to Aunt Kara's penthouse. Perfect. 53rd Avenue is just a few blocks down from Aunt Kara's place. I might have a chance at this. But then I think of all the people who were viewing the broadcast. What was the number? One million, two-thousand, eighty-three? I think. Well, I might still have a chance. I might as well try. Right? I'll ask Aunt Kara since she's like a fashion idol in New York. I might have a reputation or something.

Mark taps me on the shoulder and I see he finished the broadcast and the commercial. I tug out my ear buds and he does the same.

"What do you think?" I ask excitedly.

"You're really going to try?"

"I mean, the place is just a few blocks down from Aunt Kara's house. I mapped it."

"Well, they'll be a lot of people. From all over America. Sadie, I'm encouraging you with everything that you do, but this? I don't know."

"You think I can't do it?"

"No, Sadie. I believe in you. It's just that if you do the math, you have a," He pauses and does the math. "You have a chance of one out of one million, two-thousand, eighty-three." My face changes. "You see what I mean?" He asks.

"Yes." I sigh. "I'll ask Aunt Kara when we get to New York."

Then, Mark and I pop our ear buds in and I watch a few documentaries on sewing and the clothes that have been given awards. I watch every single documentary on sewing and sewing awards in the history of sewing. Well, maybe not all of them. Then I go to the kindle app on my phone and find a magazine on what's popular this year. I see the new style of dresses are short dresses that are made entirely out of this new material that is a mix between sequin and fleece. I see that the new style of jeans are bell bottoms. Since when? Those went out of style years ago. I keep reading. The new style in New York for fancy nights out are long dresses that trail behind you when you walk. Apparently, the casual style are short shorts with long T-shirts. Hmm. Is this magazine up to date? Whatever. I'll do what I can.

Just as I'm about to start my third fashion magazine, the flight attendant goes onto the mic and announces that we're landing in approximately five minutes. I turn off my device and get ready to land. Mark and Peter do the same. Five minutes goes by in no time and soon we start turning to one side. Then the other. Then we get level again and start our descent for landing. Finally, we hear a quiet rumble that turns into a loud booming as we land on the runway.

"Thank you for flying with Southwest. We have landed safely on the ground in New York City. The time is currently nine 'o' clock PM. We have a surprisingly cloudy night ahead of us. Enjoy your trip, everyone!"

Then the seatbelt sign turns off and we all unbuckle. Mark and Peter get out of their seats and help unload suitcases for other people on the plane. Once they grab mine and their own, we wait in line to get off the plane, Mom shortly behind.

When we finally get off the plane, we sit in the airport Carl's Junior and have somewhat of a dinner. After we finish up, Mom calls a town car to pick us up. I sit in the Carl's Junior seat at a table, pondering about my new life. I pull out my phone.

Me: Just landed and eating dinner.

Thew: Great. How's New York?

Me: We haven't even gotten out of the airport.

Thew: Ohhhh. Right. Well, I'll let you get back to it. Call me when you get a chance.

Me: :)

I put my phone back in my pocket and get out of the chair to walk to the front of the airport with Mark, Peter, and Mom. We walk past all the gates of anxious people ready for a vacation. Is this place really that bad? We finally get to the front of the airport and run right up to the town car with a person holding a bright yellow sign that reads "Benton." I hop into the back seat with Mark and Peter as Mom gets the front next to the driver. It's so late here. We departed at like eight AM and flew for what seemed like forever. So probably anywhere from seven to eight hours in the air. Then, adding the time difference, it makes it nine PM here like the flight attendant said. It's going to take a lot of getting used to.

"Where do you guys need a ride to?" The driver asks.

"Kara Calone's house, please." Mom says.

"That's private property, Mrs. Benton."

"That's my sister."

"Um. Let me make a call."

"Excuse me. I need a ride there. She's been expecting us. For days. Mr., I demand you take us there now."

"I'm just giving her a call." He responds calmly in his thick New York accent.

"Ugh." Mom sounds just like me sometimes.

I think it's time for me to say something. This is not the first time I've been to New York. When my family actually had money, we would come visit Aunt Kara for every single holiday. Literally every single holiday. We have rooms at her house and everything that she designs herself. She's seriously the best Aunt ever. But then to even get there, the driver needs to start driving. I think I remember how people operate here. Money. "Sir?"

"Yes, Miss?"

"I believe we have some extra cash in our pockets if you can get us there fast. We're late." I empty my small wallet that was stuffed inside the front pocket of my travel backpack.

The man pauses, considering my offer. "I'm just making the call."

Now, I add a little bit of Mom in there. "I demand you to take us there or we'll get a taxi to drive us there." I look behind me at the car pulled up behind our van. I see the bright yellow colors and know for sure that it's a taxi. "How about we take a taxi instead of this?" I pause. "Idiotic town car business." I finish as I start scooping up my money.

"Wait, wait, wait." He eyes me scooping up the money. "If Miss Kara really is your sister," He looks at Mom. "I'll take you guys there in a jiffy." He turns the car to motion and speeds off into the city. Works every time.

Chapter 10

New York is so pretty at night. Prettier than I remember.
I press my face against the window gently to look out at
the huge skyscrapers beside me. The lights are so
beautiful as they reflect off of the many glass windows. I
can't wait to get out there and explore. Being on the plane
for that long has me wishing to get outside and be free for
a bit. As the driver slows down at a stop light, I see the
FOTR Studio.

"Excuse me?" I say.

"Yes ma'am?" The driver answers.

"Tell me about this building here." I point to the FOTR
Studio.

"Oh. That building. They're putting on some new fashion
TV show. I believe their taking auditions this week.
Everyone here is really excited."

"Thank you."

"Yep." Then he presses his foot on the gas and we
continue speeding off to my aunt's house. Since the
FOTR Studio isn't that far away from Aunt Kara's house,
it takes less than five minutes to get there at the speed
we're going. Everyone here seems to go way faster than
they do back home. When we pull onto the driveway of
the penthouse apartment complex, the driver lets us off
and I let him take my money.

"Thank you." Then he turns the car around and speeds
away, most likely to give someone else a ride.

I grab my huge suitcase, as do Mark and Peter, off of the
sidewalk. Then, Mom pulls out her phone, clicks
something into the screen, and grabs her bag. "This way
kids." She leads us through a parking garage and to a
glass elevator. Peter walks up to the button and pushes it.
Then we wait.

"Our new life starts here." Mom tries to sound excited.

"Yay." I say, my mind somewhere else.
When the elevator finally arrives, we walk inside and
Mom pushes level twenty-five. The highest level in the
complex. The elevator shoots off into the air and I look
out the glass windows. I see a gazillion luxury houses
that my family could not ever afford, even on better days.
I also see the FOTR Studio, to what looks like just across
the street. I can't believe it's still in view from here. As
we continue our ascent, I can see at least half of the city.
Half. It's beautiful. Besides leaving my friends and Thew
behind, I think my life here might be quite pleasant.
When the elevator finally comes to a smooth halt, the
doors stay closed. I turn around and start to panic. Then
bars go over the doors.
"Authorized personnel only. Going back to level one."
Says a robotic voice. The whir of the gears from the
elevator start to turn on. Then my aunt comes running in.
She jumps up to the camera and gives it a very
unnecessary whack. The whir of the gears stops and both
the bars and the doors open smoothly.
"Welcome!" My aunt yells. She runs up to Mark and
Peter first, not bothering to wait for us to get out of the
elevator. She looks at Mark. "How are you taller than
me? This is not going to fly." Then she walks to Peter
and gives him two kisses, one on each cheek. "Last but
not least," She does a catwalk over to me. "How've you
been? I missed you."
"You're going to be tired of me pretty soon." I joke.
"Let me take you guys around the house. I've been
making some add-ons to the penthouse to make it just
right. I have a few friends that helped me with it for only
a whoppin' one hundred thousand dollars!" I gape at her.
She did make unnecessary upgrades. And even worse.
She thinks she got them for a cheap price. One hundred
thousand dollars! This is going to be insane.

"Also, sorry about the elevator. It leads straight up to my living room now and I don't want some *I-wanna-push-all-the-buttons-mommy* toddler coming in. Imagine that." She says in a mouthful. Then, she walks up to my mom. "I've got them covered, Martha." She whispers. "You go take care of yourself. Your room is upstairs. Just walk straight down the hall and make a hard left right in the center."

"Thank you, Kara." My mom cries.

"Anytime, big sis." She pats my mom on the shoulder.

 My mom rushes to the elevator on the other side of the living room to take it upstairs to what sounds like her bedroom. "C'mon kids. Welcome to the living room." She spreads her arms out wide.

As I look around, I notice she's redone her place since the last time I was here. A huge TV hangs above a luxurious fire place with a single plush couch facing it. And it's not a small couch. It's a large, white, couch that has a teal blanket draped over the side. On one side of the couch, there's a pink heart pillow. I love how the white couch matches the white surrounding walls but that the blanket and pillow are accents that stand out. Under the couch is a circular pink fur rug that matches the heart pillow exactly. It has a clear glass coffee table on it with a plant decoration and a pile of the latest fashion magazines. Aunt Kara gives us a minute to look around.

"Follow me." She yells excitedly.

We walk into the next room which appears to be her extra-large kitchen. She has a huge stove and beautiful white marble counter tops with most likely the most expensive toaster. It's literally gold. She also has a super expensive blender, tea machine, coffee machine, microwave, everything. Sitting at the stove are pots and pans all lined up in a neat line, filled up to the brim with most likely our five-star dinner.

"Then come through here." Aunt Kara says, opening a door in the back of the white kitchen.

We all walk through the door and get dumped out in a pearly white hallway. The hallway is long and has three doors on each side. "I'll wait out here while you guys go on inside. Mark, Peter, to the left. Sadie, to the right." A smile creeps up her face.

Here comes the upgrades. I walk into the third door on the right while Mark and Peter start on the first door on the left. Just as I'm about to walk into the third room, Mark and Peter both scream. I run into my room wondering what could be inside. When I walk in, I know it's not a bedroom for me but a sewing room. There's a large window used as a wall with a desk pressed against it. On the desk sits the newest sewing machine that was released last month. All around the sewing machine are pictures of my friends and family with me, my dad, Mark and Peter, Addy and Marie, and again, Thew, that my mom probably sent Aunt Kara to get printed out.

On each side of the desk, they're mannequins that I can use to pin up my clothes that I sew. I walk around the spacious room admiring the detail of the paintings hung on the wall. There's a long couch that's pressed up against a wall in the room. It has pillows and blankets over it. It's beautiful. Above it has a beautiful portrait of my family that must have been painted a long time ago because Mark and Peter were toddlers and I was just a baby. The background of the photo is beautiful. It looks like we're in a park, but not a normal park. In the background, there's cherry blossom trees and delicate white benches spread out around the park.

I walk out of the room and into the next, the second door on the right. It appears to be an office. An office for me. I can tell it's mine because over the desk hangs more photos of my family, friends, and I with an occasional S hanging around the room. The walls are almost all windows except one to hang the photos and S's. This must be where I do my school work. I take a second to admire the room and its beauty. I'm in New York and I have a feeling I'm going to be living the dream.

I walk out of the door and wonder what kind of surprises Aunt Kara added to the third door, my room. I open the door and close my eyes only to surprise myself. I open my eyes and wow; this room never gets old. I've seen it so many times in my past but I love it more each time. In my bedroom is a beautiful white bunk bed with a lace drape that hangs on the ceiling. It has a little table under my bunk bed with a new laptop computer, a phone charger and stand, and a few more photos of my family on one side and my friends on the other. On the other side of the huge room, there's another table that I can use to put some of my old stuff on from home. All the walls in my room are windows except for the one with my door, of course. I walk to the window and look out at the city. It's an even better view up here than it was in the car. I love it.

I keep walking around the room until I find myself opening the doors to my wardrobe. Something clicks when I open the doors and I almost fall into a hole and bonk my head on a pole that shoots out from it. I look down the hole and can't see a thing. Somehow, my wardrobe was replaced by a hole. Definitely some kind of an upgrade. Ok? Then I realize what it is. I grab onto the pole and slide down into the mysterious room. It's pitch black until I lower myself into the room and put my feet on the floor. The lights flash on.

"Face recognition complete." Says the robotic voice. "Welcome, Sadie."
I walk farther into the room and can make up a tiny dot in the distance that must be my wardrobe. The room is huge. And it's not just a room, it's multiple rooms. Who could need that much space? I look around the room I'm in and again realize I was blind when I entered. These rooms are my closet.

Chapter 11

All across the walls are dresses of every color from apricot to zaffre. There're short little party dresses at the very top of the twelve-foot-tall wall, and long dresses towards the bottom. In the room with all of my dresses, there's little fixtures with matching purses for every single one of the gowns or party dresses.
As I walk along the walls of the room, gently running my hand over the dresses lined up at the bottom rack. I walk all the way to the end of the room, then turn around and face my beautiful dress room behind me. Then, I walk through the doorway to the next room. It appears to be a shirt room. On one wall there are t-shirts and on the next, blouses. On the other walls, there are long sleeve sweatshirts, sweaters, jackets, coats, and everything that goes on my upper body. This time, the fixtures in the middle of the room are filled with bracelets, necklaces, and earrings. As I walk around the circular fixture, I realize that there a few empty spots for me to put my jewelry from home.
More excited with each step, I prance to the next, and final room of my closet. In this room, there are every kind of bottoms I can imagine. Pants. Shorts. More specifically, skinny jeans, ripped jeans, leggings, everything. The shorts are all different kinds too. Jean shorts, some ripped some not, biker shorts, super long shorts that are shorter than capris but longer than the normal shorts length. There are even the super short shorts that I read about in the magazine on the plane.

As I walk around the room, my hand catches on a hanger that holds a pair of the Cutest. Shorts. Ever. I turn around and try to free my hand from the hanger, but it doesn't work. I keep pulling. And pulling. And pulling. Until finally, the hanger comes off of the rack and I fly backwards. As I lay on the floor, the ground starts shaking. I think I bumped my head. I rub my head but nothing feels like I have a goose egg. Suddenly, two of the walls start shifting to just make a tiny hole big enough for me to crawl through. I stand up and walk up to the tiny hole. I poke my head under it to take a peek and see complete darkness. *Nothing to see here.* Then, as I'm taking my head out from under the hole, I see a glimmering light. What is that? I put myself in the smallest form I can get into and roll through the hole. When I reach the other side, my head really hurts this time. I haven't rolled on the ground since forever. I unravel myself from the ball I rolled into and when I look up, I see not just one gleaming light, but hundreds. I stand up slowly and walk up to the first light. In the glimmering light is a pair of leather heels. I slowly reach out and run my hand over the soft leather strap. Then, the next light starts flashing and I walk to it to find a pair of Converse high tops with blue stars all over them. Then suddenly, another light in front of me flashes and then the next one and the next and the next. Under each light lays a pair of shoes that are just my size. The lights keep flashing through the dark room and I run with them examining every detail of the shoes as a run by. *Oh, Aunt Kara. How many more surprises do you have in store?* I knew I was her favorite. There're hundreds of shoes down here in this long room, maybe more. I never want to leave this room but I know I have to get back upstairs eventually so no one comes looking for me. I walk slowly this time to admire the shoes on my way back to the little hole. I walk back to the hole and crawl through it again to get back to my main closet rooms. When I get back into the bottoms room, I pick up the hanger with a pair of shorts and put it back where it was and the walls close up the hole. Wow. I walk back to the dress room and grab a sleeping gown to change into. I then stride over to the fire pole where I came up and a small lift comes down for me to ride back up. I get back upstairs to the regular level and go into the room where I hear Mark and Peter talking.

"Hey, Sadie. Where have you been? We went through all your rooms." Mark asks.

"I was in my closet." I say proudly.

Peter makes a weird face and Mark shrugs it off. "Come look at our rooms. Aunt Kara made the smallest upgrades that turned out to leave the biggest impact!" Peter gives me a piggy back ride all the way through their three rooms. The first is a video game room with an Xbox, Nintendo Switch, and a few different Play Stations for them to mess around with. The next room is an office for both of them and the last room is the biggest. The entrance into the room is through double doors. The walls are painted blue for Mark and Peter and each of their beds are on a different side of the huge room. Honestly, it's like two of their rooms from back home combined into one. I mean, it's really huge. On the back wall, they have a huge aquarium with two snapping turtles, exactly twelve goldfish, a few sea anemones, and some other fish I don't know what to call. Literally, instead of a whole wall being a window, like in my bedroom, they have a whole wall made out of a fish tank. How is that *little*, Peter? Crazy.

My aunt comes into the room and announces that it's time for bed. I guess we need to get into the New York schedule. I hug Mark and Peter goodnight and walk into my room. I see my wardrobe is back from its long journey through my closet and I change into the comfy sleeping gown and walk up to the wardrobe, old clothes in hand. To get my clothes into the closet downstairs, I need to open my wardrobe quickly, stuff the clothes in, and close the doors immediately as to not make the wardrobe disappear and reappear as a fire pole. Right? If I do it quick enough, it might work. I open the doors super-fast, stuff my clothes in, and slam the doors shut. The wardrobe zips down into my floor and becomes replaced with the fire pole. Ugh. This might take some getting used to. My aunt startles me by coming in and saying, "You know there's a dirty clothes bin." She points to a bin right next to where the wardrobe usually sits. "I see you've found your closet." She sits on my bed and pats the spot next to her, motioning for me to sit down next to her.

I sit down next to her and respond "Yeah. It's pretty great down there. And by the way, I found my shoe closet, too." I smile.

"Good. I thought you might like it."

"How long did it take to make all that? The fire pole and the tall walls and stuff?"

"Oh, well…" She thinks for a second. "I put in a bit of extra money if they could do it in a week."

My mouth drops open. "A week? A *week*?" I scream. "That's so unrealistic."

"I know. I know."

"And how much money do you even have? In my whole life, I wouldn't even have enough money to have a penthouse in New York. But somehow you *do* have a penthouse in New York *with* a super huge closet that goes into the apartment under us." I grasp for air.

My aunt just laughs. "I know. It *is* pretty unbelievable. Just like I said though, one hundred thousand dollars and a little peck on the cheek from me can do a lot." She winks. "Money isn't everything and that is important to understand, but one thing I learned on my journey to fame and fortune was that people, particularly our family, tend to underestimate themselves. We can do huge things we can't even imagine. We just have to try, and if we fail, we can't give up. It's a wonderful thing to dream big and go after it".

"Really?" My mouth says without following the instructions to be quiet from my brain. "You know, there's a sewing contest for tweens my age that's going to be streaming all over America. I want to join but I thought I'd ask you. They're taking auditions at the FOTR studio just a block or two down." *Shut up, mouth.*

"Oh really? I haven't heard. You should try. You're really excellent at sewing."

"You think?"

"Oh yes. I know."

I pull out my phone and get to a photo I took of myself wearing the silk dress I sewed and show it to my aunt. "I sewed this a few weeks ago using the fabric you got me for my birthday."

My aunt snatches the phone out of my hand and zooms in to look at the dress closely. When she does, her eyes practically bulge out of her head. "You…" She can barely make words, it seems. "You sewed this?"

"Yes. I didn't think it was *that* good-"

"That good? That *good*?" My aunt sounds like me more than Mom ever can. I guess we *are* related. "Sadie Benton, you are submitting this to the audition and you will make it in. No matter what."

Chapter 12

The next morning, I wake up bright and early to my aunt coming in and jumping on my bed. "I'm still trying to sleep." I whine. She's never grown up and she never will. "I'm taking you to the auditions early today so we can be the first in line." She yells excitedly.
Turns out, we're the four-hundred-and-twenty-sixth people in line.
"So much for coming early." I yawn. My aunt is practically bouncing to the ceiling so I decide to give my complaints a rest. I look ahead at the huge line and make out tons and tons of kids my age with their parents, some maybe with their grandparents. Mark and Peter said they would stop by at twelve-thirty to give us lunch. Behind the check-in stand outside the studio, there's huge lines of people still trying to get into the studio. I'm so happy that I'm the four-hundred-and-twenty-sixth person in line and not the one-millionth person. I really didn't know this audition would be so huge. I mean, it *is* New York City. I pull out my phone and walk over to a bench outside. It's best to get some fresh air every once and a while. I click on Thew's contact and press *video chat.* He answers almost immediately and I see he's on the school bus with his friends in his normal seat at the front of the bus.
"Hey, Sadie." They all yell in unison.
"Hi, everyone." I say.
"How've you been? How's life in New York?" Thew asks.
"It's really great. Right now, I'm in line for an audition for this new TV show that's coming out next week."
"You'll be a star." Squeaks Pip, one of Thew's friends that I've gotten to know really well.
"Well, first I have to get through the auditions. Then, I might just be able to wing it to the finals."

"Finals?" Addy pops her head out from the seat behind
Thew.
"Well, it's a sewing competition that's taking contestants
from all across the US." I explain.
Marie pops her head out from the seat behind Pip. "You
mean the Fashion on the Run one?"
"Yep."
"You'll totally make it." Addy says excitedly.
"Well, if I do the calculations," Marie leans back in her
seat and you can see her thinking super hard, just like
Mark.
"What number, exactly, are you in line?" Bruce asks,
another of Thew's friends that I've gotten to know.
I hold up the laminated sheet of paper that hangs around
my neck.
"Four-hundred-and-twenty-six?" Marie screams.
I nod sadly. "I might, just might, still be able to get it."
"You've got this Sadie. We've got to go now. Sorry to
cut it short." says Thew.
"Already? Well, bye guys." I say sadly. It was nice to get
to see all my friends again, even on the phone. It just
went by really fast. I turn off my phone and take a deep
breath of the New York air. Then, I walk back inside to
where Aunt Kara stands, holding my place in line.
"Did you remember it?" Aunt Kara asks.
"Remember what?" I say back.
"The dress. That you're entering for the audition?" She
goes on.
I slap myself on the forehead. "I completely forgot. It's
packaged on a box that's on a truck that's on its way
here." I take a deep breath, telling myself it'll still be fine.
"Ugh." I scream, losing my temper quickly.
"Sadie." My aunt looks at me. "You should've told me."
"I'll never do it." I scream even louder. This time people
look at me.

"Pipe down now. You'll just have to sew something else for them to see."

"Them?" My mind races.

"Yes, *them*. The judges."

"The judges?" My mind has officially gone crazy.

"Sadie, when there's a sewing competition, there's always judges." My aunt says calmly.

"Yep. Yep. Judges. Judges. Who?"

"The *judges.*"

"Who? Who are the judges?" I start hyper ventilating. Mark might have been right. What are my chances? I didn't even bring my dress and now I have to face some crazy fashionista judges. I knew there were judges, I just never really thought about them as a problem. Until now.

"Sadie, calm down. It'll be alright. You're a great seamstress and you know it. You just have to do what you do at home. I'm sure you'll get in if you set your mind to it."

"My mind? My mind has gone crazy. I can't do it with all these other four-hundred-and-twenty-five people in front of me. Why would they try to come all this way to New York if they weren't good?"

"She has a point." A lady in front of me says, putting a comforting arm around her daughter. Her daughter turns around and looks at me.

"You alright?" The daughter asks me. She has a thick country accent so I assume she's from somewhere in the South. "I'm kind of scared too. I didn't know there'd be this many people."

I drop my face so no one can read what I'm thinking, like she clearly just did.

"I'm Trinity, but for some reason, my friends call me Tiny. What's yours?" She asks.

"This is my niece, Sadie." My aunt fills in for me. "And you are?" My aunt asks Tiny's mom.

"I'm Harriet. Oh-my-word!" Harriet stutters as she turns fully around to greet my aunt and I.

Tiny looks up at my aunt and her eyes grow wide. "Oh, my gee willigers. You're Kara Calone?" She grabs my aunt's hand and shakes it rapidly.

"Well, yes. I am."

"How could I ever be in presence of you without knowing it?" Tiny says excitedly. "You're like, the goddess of fashion." Tiny squeals. Harriet nods in agreement.

"Well. I'm. Glad. That. I. Could. Meet. You." My aunt tries to say but the fast movement from Tiny shaking her hand affects the way she talks. It makes me look up and I suppress a laugh. My aunt folds her hand into a fist and slips out of Tiny's death grip on her hand.

"Oh, sorry ma'am." Tiny looks ashamed.

"Where are you from?" I suddenly ask, trying to take the conversation off of my aunt so she could get a minute to re-cooperate.

"Well look who's talk 'n now?" Tiny says. "I'm from Lexington, Kentucky." Then she goes on and on and on about her hometown and her pet horse and the farm she works on. It's probably for the better because it makes the line go by faster. When she finally finishes, there's only five people in front of us. Phew. "Do you have any pets?" She asks.

"Sadly, no. I wish I had a dog."

"Aww. What'll you name yer pupper?"

"Good question. I haven't really thought about it." I say,

"Well, I'm darn tootin'n sure your pupper will be a queen with you guys around. Got any siblings? I got thirteen but I'm the second oldest."

"Thirteen? I have two siblings. I'm the youngest." I
respond.
"You're pretty old to be the youngest." She laughs.
"I guess so." I say,
"Do you get a room to yourself?" She asks suddenly.
"Not to brag, but yes. Three in fact."
"Three? All to yourself?"
"Yep."
"Wowsers. I have to share mine with Timmy, Tommy,
Sara Lee, Clark, Francis, Laura, and Mary Pat. The other
five have to share the other one. My older sibling, Sonata,
she moved out as soon as she was old enough."
"Sonata? I actually know a Sonata that works at a
pancake place by my old house. She talks like you too, no
offense. Do you think that's her?"
"I bet you Sonata does live near you! She sends a phone
call every once and a while and says she does work at a
pancake place! I never knew that she lived near
somebody like you!"
"Haha. Well, it was my old place. But back to you, how
do you even sleep with all those kids in your room?" I
start to feel more comfortable talking to her now that we
have a common ally.
It's taken some practice to share the room ever since
Sonata left. There's laugh'n and fart'n all night long.
When Sonata was there, she didn't take any of that and
had a way to make 'em stop laugh'n and fart'n." I make a
face. "Too much? Sorry."
"It's fine."
"NEXT." A loud voice booms and Tiny turns around and
starts walking to the door.
"Bye y'all." She says to me.

"Good luck." I say back. Then my nerves start kicking in again. What if I don't make it? I need it. I need the money. I'm not good enough for this. Inhale, exhale, inhale, exhale.

"Sadie, come on. You're going to be great. Just do what you normally do." Aunt Kara says.

"I can't do this. I'm leaving right now." I make a beeline for the door but Aunt Kara grabs onto the collar of my new shirt from my closet before I can even take a step.

"I don't think so, young lady. You're staying right here until you're called. Then you walk inside and sew. I'll wait out here. Easy?"

The word *sew* helps me calm down a little bit. "Easy." I breathe in and out again to calm down. *Easy.*

A few minutes go by until the loud voice booms again. "NEXT."

"Thank you." I run up to Aunt Kara and give her a huge squeeze around the waist. Then I run up to the man guarding the door to the audition room and he takes my number necklace off of me and scans the back of it. Then he talks into his little microphone that's held on by his ear and the doors to the audition room slide slowly open. I walk inside.

Chapter 13

I hear the doors close slowly behind me and I see a huge stage in front of me. A single table with a sewing machine sits in the center of the stage. I walk onto the stage reluctantly and sit down at the little machine table. "Is this number four-hundred-and-twenty-six?" I hear Ashley's voice from above me. I've heard that voice so many times on YouTube that I would recognize it anywhere.

"Yes. Sadie Benton." A spotlight turns on and shines directly over me. It's hot. Like, real hot.

"You may present your skill." she says,

I nod and see a huge bin of fabrics to the right of the table and I stick my hand into it. My head races back to the magazines and documentaries I either read or watched on the plane. Bell bottom jeans. What was the shirt? I think it was long sleeve but I can't quite remember. I dig through the bin until I find a fancy gold fleece material. I grab it and feel it softly gliding around on my hands. Well, since I can't remember what the trendy shirt style was, what about I combine the bell bottom jean style into a shirt. I grab the scissors laying on the desk and start cutting away to a pattern I just made up in my head. I cut two identical pieces of what my shirt will be and I turn them inside out and sew it together. When, I finish sewing them together, I make sure to leave the sleeves unsewn as to give it a bell bottom type style. I turn it back to the outside and sew a trim over the seams to give it a stylish effect. After a few more minutes of cutting off random strings and fixing unsewn spots that were supposed to be sewed, I step back from the machine with the shirt in my hand.

"You may go to the dressing rooms." Ashley says. Then, the spotlight moves to a door at the back of the stage and I walk inside. I take off my old shirt and put the new shirt on. It fits just like how I wanted it too. A perfect crop top with long sleeves unsewn at the very end. In the dressing rooms, there's different bottoms I can choose from as well as accessories that I can use to show off my shirt. I take off my ripped shorts and put on a pair of the most stylish bell bottom jeans I see. I grab a set of emerald earrings and an emerald necklace to make an accent that matches my eyes. I slip on a pair of cork strap heels and grab a handbag to make it look like I just got back home from shopping. *Home.* The whole reason I'm doing this is to get back home. I grab some flashy gold sunglasses on my way out and place them on my head. Then, I fling the door open for my grand debut.

I walk out slowly to the front of the stage giving Ashley and the other judges some time to examine my outfit. Then, I walk back to the door and back to the front of the stage. When I finish my catwalk, all that I hear is the scribbling of a pencil and then the pencil dropping back onto the table. Another spotlight turns on and shines a light directly on Ashley and the two other judges, a man and a woman. "Thank you. You may hang up your design on a hanger as well as your other clothes back in the dressing room and exit the building." Ashley doesn't sound anything like she does on YouTube. She sounds grumpy and unsatisfied, unlike her usual bubbly self on her live streams. While taking off my shoes, I notice a bright pink sticky note stuck to the bottom. I peel it off of the shoe and read it. *If you want in the show, it will cost you. Meet me backstage.* I study the note closely and I'd recognize that handwriting anywhere. It's Ashley. *Ashley? Seriously?* Is this competition even real?

I grab the note and stick it my pocket to show Aunt Kara.
I walk slowly down the stage and exit the building,
slamming the door behind me. Aunt Kara runs up and
gives me a huge squeeze.
"Tell me *all* about it." She says with excitement. We
walk back to her limo where her personal driver, Ronald
awaits us. I notice that when she walks, she has a skip in
her step. I feel bad telling her about my failure but she
asked for it. So, I do. I tell her about my shirt and the
accents and everything. "Why do you look so down?
Your outfit sounded great." She exclaims.
"I thought it was great, but then I found a note in
Ashley's handwriting saying that it would cost me to get
into the show."
"What? How do you know that? Are you sure it was from
Ashley?" She asks.
"Yes, the note was stuck to my shoe." I respond glumly.
"Oh sweetie."
"I feel dumb because I should have known that this
wasn't a real competition about talent. They're looking
for competitors that *pay* to be in the show." I yell.
"Don't be too hard on yourself. Maybe there is some
misunderstanding. The guard at the door told me the
FOTR mail truck will deliver your results later today.
You still have a chance, sweetie, even if we don't pay.
We'll get to the bottom of this, don't worry." She says as
she takes the folded note from my pocket.
"A chance of one out of one million, two-thousand,
eighty-three." I yell even louder, repeating Mark's words.
As I hop into the extra-long car, a staff member at the
FOTR Studio comes and knocks on my window. Ronald
rolls down my window and the staff member starts
talking.

"Make sure to turn on the FOTR channel on TV at four to see the stats of the auditions so you don't have to wait for the mail."

"Roll up the window." I tell the Ronald.

"But wait. There's more. Wait!" The staff member yells as the window rolls up and Ronald speeds off deep into the city of New York.

I sit in the very back of the limo because there are huge candy dispensers and TVs. I turn on the TV to the FOTR channel, just to see what's on. I stuff myself with M&M's and Reese's Pieces as the TV slowly loads and connects to the internet while we're on the road. When the TV finishes connecting, I literally spit out my candy. They're filming the auditions. I made myself a public humiliation. And not just neighbors and friends will see that but all of America. *America.* I rewind the live TV channel to when I walk onto the stage and say my name. I see my hand dig through the bin of fabrics and pull out the stupid gold fleece. I see myself think super hard and then start randomly cutting some random thing. I see myself sashay across the stage to the fitting room and the camera goes to Ashley. Happy, bubbly, *fake* Ashley.

"What a design! Can you see potential? Let me know by commenting on my livestream on YouTube." The camera cuts back to me. The TV plays some fashion model music and it shows me cat walking down the stage and back to the dressing room. I thought I was doing a catwalk but I looked like a zombie mixed with some flying pony doing some weird prance across the stage. I took some awkward curtsey that I don't even remember doing and then it cuts straight to me slump walking off the stage and to the exit. It even plays fake applause sounds in the background. It makes me look like some unappreciative girl that hates fame and didn't even want to audition in the first place. In other words, they made me look stupid.

I fast forward the program back to the current contestant and watch for a while as Ronald takes us deep into the city of New York. The current contestant designs a cute but stylish jean dress and matches it with a pair of black heels and a brown braided belt. She wears a flower headband and walks casually out to the front of the stage and the fake applause starts. The girl looks exactly my age and is so much better at sewing than me. The next contestant is a boy who designs a tie using a nice red plaid fabric. When he gets back out from the dressing room, he does a professional catwalk out to the front of the stage and once again, the fake applause takes over the fashion music. He gives the camera a smile and when the camera zooms in on his face, I recognize him from the cover of one of the magazines I read on the plane. Who knew models design clothes? The next few people are all girls about my age. They design cute little dresses or shorts that they rip using seam rippers. After a while, no one really strikes my eye except for an older girl, maybe sixteen, who designs a beautiful pair of jean shorts that somehow have a wavy flow to them. I don't know how she did it, but she did it very well. It wasn't just the shorts though; it was whenever she walked out of the dressing room wearing her pair of flowy jean shorts and my shirt. *Mine.* That I sewed. I give myself a pleased smile and hope that she at least makes it onto the show.

When we finally arrive into town, my aunt hops out of the front seat and I hop out of the back.

"Thanks, Ronald." Aunt Kara says to the driver.

Ronald goes to park in a garage nearby while my aunt takes me down the avenue, arms linked. Aunt Kara knows I have nothing to say so we walk a little way silently, which makes my stomach hurt, until we get to a shop called Mademoiselle Made.

We walk inside and head straight to the first fixture in front of us. It's complete with shoes, earrings, necklaces, and a few handbags. "How many things can a store have on one display?" I whisper to no one in particular. The rest of the handbags are on a rack at the back of the store. My aunt picks up a pair of heels that are made entirely out of cork but have a bright red leather strap. She turns them over to check the price.

"They also have great deals here." She says.

I peek over her shoulder at the price tag on the bottom of the shoe. Two-hundred-and-twenty-five dollars. That's a rip off. Then, my eyes drift off to a pair of heels next to the ones my aunt found. They're all made of cork, just like my aunt's, except the strap is made of a luminescent pink that would match my silk dress exactly. I grab them before even thinking and flip them over to see the price. This time, Aunt Kara peeks over my shoulder. She grabs them out of my hand and throws them into her shopping bag before I even have time to look at the price. "Done." she says.

"How much were they?" I ask.

"Don't bother." Before I have time to argue, she grabs my arm again and pulls me to the clothes rack to the left of the fixture we were shopping at.

This goes on for hours and hours at each different shop we go to down the avenue. After we're done shopping, we head to lunch. I have a total of eight shopping bags, four on each arm, and my aunt has ten bags, five on each arm.

We walk around this fancy food court area for a while so I can figure out what I want to eat. I decide on a plain cheeseburger, just the meat, the cheese, and the bun. My aunt gets a nutritious salad that she says is her favorite. She says her other favorite is the pizza and that I should try it sometime. I make a mental note on trying a slice of pizza from *Susie's*, the place we're eating at.

Around three o' clock, my aunt calls Ronald and a minute later, he shows up at our sides and welcomes us aboard. I load the shopping bags into the empty seats next to me and pull out my phone. Mark texted that he couldn't figure out how to use the stove so he couldn't bring us lunch. I told him it was fine and that we just had lunch, so he shouldn't worry. I put my phone up and look out at the beautiful New York City, just outside the window. All the way back to my new home, I stare out the window at all of the beautiful sights to see. It's perfect. The only thing that's missing is Addy, Marie, and Thew.

When Ronald pulls up at the driveway of the penthouse complex, he lets us out and calls a butler to help us carry our shopping bags. We walk to the elevator, the butler slowly trailing behind us, and press the up button. The elevator comes whirring down a few seconds later and the three of us board the elevator. The robotic face scanner scans my aunt's face and we walk through the doors to the living room, now full of old brown boxes. My aunt instructs the butler to leave the bags on the floor and exit. She gives him a "small" tip of thirty dollars and he goes back down the elevator. Mark and Peter walk into the room just in time to see the look on Aunt Kara's and my face. This room needs work.

"Boxes arrived." Peter says happily as he grabs two or three boxes labeled PETER on it. He carries them through the door that leads straight to the hallway and I hear the sound of Peter dropping boxes on his floor. He appears again into the living room and does the same thing. This happens repeatedly so my aunt and I join in. My aunt helps carry my mom's stuff to her room and I carry the boxes labeled SADIE. I take two boxes, all that my arms can carry, into my room and head back into the living room to grab more. I get into the pattern and soon only twenty or so boxes are left at exactly three fifty-five so Mark, Peter, and Mom join me on the couch as I press the TV on and turn the channel to FOTR. Aunt Kara goes to the door to look for my letter that should be arriving any minute now.

Chapter 14

The TV shows the FOTR mail truck zip off and go straight to the hotel where all the auditioners were required to stay if they were from out of town. After the mail man leaves with three quarters of the letters out of his bag, he's off again delivering the rest of the mail to the local auditioners. I suddenly run to the window like I'm eight years old and anxiously waiting for an ice cream truck to drive by. I sit there for a few minutes before the unmistakable bright pink FOTR truck pulls into the driveway to deliver someone's letter. *My* letter. If this contest is legit, this could change my life. I try to think positive. I could be famous and be able to have enough money to buy back our old house. My life could be changed in the best way possible. My life, is in that envelope. The elevator pulls up to the living room with the FOTR mail man in it.
"Did you not see the mail slot?" Aunt Kara asks impatiently.
"Um. No. Sorry mam."
"I'm messing with you. Now hand over that letter."
The guy quickly gives Aunt Kara the letter and spams the down button, ready to leave this place. Aunt Kara prances over to me and hands me the letter. Then, she sits down next to my mom on my right, Mark and Peter on my left. I tear open my letter and read the bright black letters:

FAILED

Everyone's smiles immediately drop and I become the middle of a huge ball of warmth and comfort from my family who jump up to surround me. How could I have failed? Well, I guess I do know. The whole contest was fake, just like Ashley. The channel changes to a ranking list of first, second, third, fourth, and fifth. The little eleven-year-old made it in second, and some other people I didn't watch made it on. I feel sorry for Tiny because now she has to go back home to her ranch telling all her younger siblings that she had to leave because she was a failure. Like me. The TV cuts to Ashley talking in front of the studio about how *sorry* she was for the people that didn't make it on and how she still had auditions tomorrow for the rest of the line that they didn't have time for today. Suddenly, Aunt Kara jumps up.

"Sadie, Mark, Peter, go search for Sadie's silk dress. Martha, come with me." My aunt says to my mom with urgency. I don't know what kind of plan my aunt has, but sounds like we need to do exactly as we're told. Mark, Peter, and I run into my room to search through the boxes while my mom and Aunt Kara run into another room to do something. Mark starts on a box in the far-right corner of my room and gently unpacks it while Peter unpacks a box on the far left of my room and practically breaks the box with such force, it takes him less than thirty seconds to rip out all of my things. I start in the middle of my room and unload things carefully, but fast. After I go through about three of my boxes, Peter starts screaming.

"Over here. Found it. Found it."

I run over to the box and swiftly pull out my silk dress and bow. I run into the living room with Mark and Peter and we start yelling for Aunt Kara and Mom. They run into the room and Aunt Kara instructs me to get dressed into it. I don't bother asking why and I run into my room. Mark and Peter follow me back into my room and I pull open the doors to my wardrobe and the fire pole appears. "Hold this." I throw the dress into Marks arms and slide down the fire pole. Peter comes down right after me, needing no invitation and Mark throws me the dress and slides down too.

"Let us *all* in." I command the robot. She listens and lets us all enter my closet. I run straight to the very last room and pull the hanger off the rack and the little door opens. Mark and Peter are still surprised from the fact that I have my own secret closet, so when I crawl into the hole, I can feel their faces change. I rip off my clothes and gently put on my dress. I run towards the middle of the shoe room where I remember there being a cute pair of white heels. I find them and run back out the tiny hole.

"Let's go." I say,

I walk quickly as to not ruin my dress up to the fire pole. The little lift comes down and the three of us walk onto it.

"That was sooooo cool." Peter yells as we arrive back on the main level.

"I know." I say, I run into my bathroom I haven't quite explored yet and find a bag of hair ties in a drawer on my vanity. I put my hair in a neat pony tail and then braid my hair off of the ponytail. I finish the braid by tying the bow in the back of my hair. I run slowly into the living room where my aunt and mom are standing.

"Perfect." My aunt squeals.

"What exactly are we doing?" I ask.

"No time to explain. Get in the car." She sticks her hand in a shopping bag and pulls out a silk handbag she bought me. She tosses it to me and I jump into the elevator. Mark and Peter jump in next to me and my aunt grabs her phone and hops in too.

My mom stays in the room glued to the TV. My aunt now spams the down button and the elevator starts moving downwards at the same speed it normally goes. Aunt Kara still thinks it'll go faster if she keeps pressing the button. We suddenly come to a halt at level two and the doors open. Two teenagers, a girl and a boy start to come on the elevator.

"Use the stairs for goodness sake." Aunt Kara yells at them. She pulls us all out of the elevator and ushers us down the stairs. When we finally get to the bottom, Aunt Kara hops in the back of the limo with Mark, Peter, and I. My aunt turns on the TV to the FOTR channel and watches intensely.

Ashley is still outside blabbing on and on about how beautiful the winners' designs were. Aunt Kara stuffs herself with a ton of gummy bears while at the same time brushing her hair and reapplying makeup.

"You two stay in the car. Sadie, when we get there, you're coming with me."

The limo speeds off going way faster than it should be until we pull up at the FOTR studio. We come to a screeching halt and Aunt Kara jumps out of the car. On the TV in the car, you can tell the cameraman turned his head to see what the commotion was about, bringing the camera with him. All that you see on screen is an angry Aunt Kara coming out of a limo. She grabs my hand and I end up jumping out of the car as well. Ashley is tapping the cameraman's shoulder to make him face her but he refuses and keeps the camera on Aunt Kara and I.

"You nut job. You think you're so smart." Aunt Kara accuses Ashley. Aunt Kara stares directly into the camera lenses. This isn't her first time on camera. "All you contestants out there, I'm talking to you."

Ashley taps rapidly on the cameraman's shoulder and loudly whispers "Commercial break. Commercial break." Aunt Kara keeps talking. "All you contestants who didn't make it in is because you guys didn't PAY to get on the show." She pauses and sternly looks directly at Ashley. "Yep. That's right. One person has ruined this entire experience for all of you young and talented designers. This is my niece, Sadie Benton. She auditioned but didn't get in because she refused to buy her way into this show. This lady here," Aunt Kara directs the cameraman to Ashley. "She is a dream killer." Ashley's trying to suppress a smile but you can tell it's fake. "I demand that you let my niece into this competition and let all of the other contestants who didn't make it in audition again and fairly!"

"I'm sorry but I can't do that. The votes are already in." Ashley tries to say calmly.

"What votes?" My aunt screams. "I know how TV works. It's all about you. You're the star. You get to decide who's in or out. Not votes."

"Mam, I have to ask you to leave." Ashley says a little less calm and more scared.

"Do you even know who I am? What kind of fashionista are you if you're asking me to leave? I *am* fashion." My aunt says strongly. The camera man faces Aunt Kara again.

"Mam, of course I know who you are." Ashley responds vaguely.

"Well then, who am I?"

"Martha Benton." Ashley says coolly.

"Martha Benton? *Martha Benton*?" Aunt Kara screams even louder.

"Of course, mam. Sadie Benton is your daughter."

"My name is NOT Martha Benton. I am Kara Calone, Sadie's aunt, thank you very much."

"Of course." Ashley sounds super scared now.

"All you contestants who didn't make it on this show, get back here. The shows not over just yet." The camera man goes to commercial break as Ashley stomps back inside the FOTR studio crying. Mark and Peter jump out of the car and hug Aunt Kara first, then me.

"Thank you, Aunt Kara." Now it's my turn to give her a squeeze.

"Anytime." She says, still steaming.

The camera goes live and the cameraman takes charge.

"Tell me about your dress." He says, filling in for the place Ashley should be doing.

"Well, one night, back in my hometown, I got back from school one day filled with, well, mixed feelings about life. My mom and dad had just gotten a divorce earlier that day and school had a lot of down sides."

"Oh no." The cameraman prompts me.

"Sewing always helped me with my emotions so I started sewing this dress. I skipped dinner and sewed all through the night. It turns out it was worth it." I give the camera a little twirl of my dress.

"It's beautiful." Says the cameraman.

"Thank you." I say,

"Tell me about these folks over here." He points to Mark, Peter, and Aunt Kara.

"Well, these are my two brothers, Mark and Peter. Mark was actually one of the main reasons I felt so confident about this dress. I would have never been here today if it weren't for him." I smile.

Mark gives a smile too. "I just saw the light in her room on at, like, one in the morning and wondered what was going on. I walked in and she was spinning around with the dress in her arms."

"Well, how lucky are you?" The cameraman asks.

"Very."

"And what were you doing?" The cameraman asks Peter.

"I was sleeping. What else would I be doing at one in the morning on a school night?" He jokes.

"Now tell me about your aunt, would you?"

"Well, this is my Aunt Kara. After my parents got a divorce, my mom, Martha, was having trouble finding a job and a few weeks later, we couldn't pay for our house. Aunt Kara took us all into her place and that's where we've been staying."

"Not to get personal, but how's your mom doing?"

"Oh, she's fine." I say, "Actually, she's at Aunt Kara's house now, probably still glued to the TV like she was when we left." I wave at the camera. *Hi Mom* and then giggle a little bit.

"Well, a big shout out to you, Mom." The cameraman says. "Oh my. Well, look at that." I turn around and see dozens and dozens of taxis pulling up at the studio with doors opening and kids filing out.

"They must be here for the auditions." I whisper in awe.

"Indeed, they are." Says the cameraman excitedly.

I give a grin as Tiny runs out of one of the taxis and gives me a huge hug. "Hey, ya'll." She waves at my brothers and Aunt Kara.

"Tell me about this friend of yours." The cameraman asks to get my attention again. He's good at this.

"Well, this is Trinity." I say, "I met her in line for the auditions."

"Well, hello there, Trinity."

"Hey ya'll." She says to the camera. "My friends call me Tiny for short. It's easier to say."

"Well then, hello Tiny."

She nods her head and gives me another squeeze. Soon all of the kids are out of there taxis and are gathering around my family and I. It's time for me to take charge. "Thanks for coming back, everyone." I yell to the crowd. "Now, don't spend your time out here because you have some auditions to get to." Everyone walks into the studio and Tiny gives me one last squeeze and joins the others inside the studio.

"Thank you so much, Sadie Benton. We're looking forward to seeing you on the show." The cameraman says. My family and I get together and wave to the camera as the livestream ends.

Chapter 15

The cameraman sets down his camera and wipes the sweat off his forehead.

"You're so good at that." I say to the cameraman.

"Thank you, Sadie. Years and years of filming Ashley, you sort of get the hang of it." He jokes.

"I bet so. What's your name?"

"I'm Brandon."

"Well, guess what, Brandon?" My aunt pipes in.

"Yes, mam?"

"You're the new host of FOTR."

"What?" Brandon says.

"Aunt Kara, I don't think you have control over that." I say kindly.

"Well, look around." She answers. I turn my head and see Ashley speed off in her bright yellow Lamborghini.

"Ok. I guess, you're right." I tell Aunt Kara.

"I'll personally see to it that Ashley never works in this business again" Aunt Kara says with a wink.

"Wow. I don't think I can do it." Brandon says.

"I'm sure you can. You're great at this kind of thing." I tell him as Brandon's assistant grabs the camera and starts filming the new host.

"Now get in there. You have some auditions to get to." Aunt Kara yells, adding opera to the end of the last sentence.

As Brandon walks through the doors to the stage, the man and the woman who were judging the contestants earlier walk out towards me. The woman introduces herself, "Hi Sadie, I'm Jane and this is Henry." She says motioning to the male judge. "We both thought your design earlier was fabulous. We both want you in the show, just like we did earlier, and are looking forward to seeing what you come up with next!"

I can hardly contain my smile as I thank the judges as we hop back into the limo and speed off back to the house. When I walk into the living room, I feel like I'm on cloud nine. Mom runs up to me and gives me a huge hug.

"You guys did great." She smiles.

"Thanks." I say.

"Look at the scores on the TV." Mom says excitedly.

I walk over to the TV and see the scoreboard. Instead of rankings, there's just names and photos of the people who made it onto the show. I'm so excited I can hardly breathe. I plop onto the couch, Mark, Peter, and Aunt Kara next to me. Just think, I could win this competition. I really have a chance now. I can do this. I pull out my phone and text my friends. They should be out of school now.

Me: Turn to channel FOTR.

Marie: Is it on already?

Me: Just look. Rewind to about twenty minutes ago.

Marie: Yay.

I click out of Marie's messages and click on Thew's.

Me: Turn to channel FOTR

Thew: Is that the competition? The one you're auditioning for?

Me: Just check. Rewind back like twenty minutes ago.

Thew: Got it on.

Lastly, I exit out of his messages and click on Addy's.

Me: Turn to channel FOTR.

Addy: I'm already watching. I saw your aunt and you and the Tiny girl. You did great.

Me: Thanks. I wish you were here with me.

Addy: Same here. But I mean like, I want to be in New York with you. I'm not big on shopping but I think I'd like to shop there.

Me: You'd like it a lot. Everything's really expensive though.

Addy: I have an allowance of twenty-five dollars a month.
I could buy a pair of shoes or two.
Me: They're like two-hundred dollars each.
Addy: LOL
Me: Seriously.
Addy: : (
Me: I'll make a group chat with you, Marie, Thew, and I
and then I'll call you guys.
Addy: Sounds good to me.

I press the plus button in the corner next to Addy's name
and create a group with the four of us. I wait a few
minutes to let Marie and Thew get caught up on what
happened.

Me: I'm letting them get caught up.
Addy: Alrighty.
Me: Can you believe my aunt?
Addy: She reminds me of you. So yeah. Kind of.
Me: Really? Of me?
Addy: Yeah. Seriously.

Me: I'll take that as a complement. :)

I press the call button in the new group chat and everyone
answers. How I miss them.

"Hey, Sade." Thew says.

"We miss you." Marie adds.

"I miss you guys too." I respond.

"We saw what happened on TV." Marie exclaims.

"Your aunt is that fashion lady?" Thew asks.

"Yes. Can you believe what she did? For me?" I say.

"Like I said before, she reminds me of you. You would
do it for us." Addy jumps in.

"For sure. You wouldn't let us down." Thew adds.

"I miss you guys so much." I tell them.

"We miss you too." They all say in unison.

"Oh my gosh. I need to show you guys my closet."

"Lead the way." Says Marie excitedly. I remember her small closet full of clothes she doesn't have room for. She wears them all though.

I turn my camera around. "So, this is my room." I say, "The view is great." Addy exclaims.

"Really great." Thew says. "I think Marie is speechless."

I laugh. "You guys haven't seen anything." I open my wardrobe doors and it descends underground to reveal the fire pole.

"I want that." Addy yells through the phone.

"Just wait." I respond. I slide down the super long pole and into my magenta closet.

"I *love* the pink." Marie says.

"Mine would be black." Addy says.

"I wouldn't care what color mine was." Thew laughs.

I slowly walk into the room showing them the twelve-foot-tall walls decked out with dresses.

"I love that purple one. Or the blue one. No. The yellow one." Marie squeals.

"You would look good in the green one." Thew chimes in.

"For sure." Addy responds.

"Yes." Marie says out of breath.

"This is just the first room." I say happily.

"There's *more*?" Addy says, gasping for air.

I keep walking into the next room, showing them all of my shirts, and sweatshirts, and jackets.

"I like the black sweatshirt." Addy says.

"I like the pink one with the bunny." Marie exclaims.

"You're liking the pink stuff." I say to Marie.

"It's my favorite color." She adds.

"I thought it was purple?" Addy and I say simultaneously.

"That too." Marie says shyly.

"Then the last room," I walk to the last one.

"This is my room." Addy says. "I'm packing right now and living in your closet."
"I don't know if the house would be down with that." I laugh.
"The house?" Addy asks.
"There's this robot that talks and doesn't let unknown people into the house." I explain.
"It's like a spy movie." Thew jokes.
"Yeah, it kind of is." We all start laughing. I walk up to the hanger and pull it off of the rack to reveal the shoe room. "This is the best part."
"Is it where you find the thief?" Thew asks curiously.
"What?" I say.
"Are you still on the spy thing?" Addy asks him.
"I thought we were still doing that." Thew says. We all start laughing again.
"To answer your question, no. This is where we find my shoes." I smile and crawl through the hole.
Marie gasps and nearly faints. "No way. I'm dying."
"Sick." Addy says.
"Wow. How many rooms are even in this house?"
"Don't know. I've only been around the main level and my closet. There's still an upstairs where my aunt and mom sleep."
"Sick." Addy says again. As I walk through the dark room with only the spotlights guiding me, I know Addy is pretending not to like shoes but I can tell she's intrigued. This time, I walk all the way to the end of the shoe room which feels like at least a mile.
"You got your exercise in for today." Thew jokes.
"For sure." Addy agrees.
"I'm still dying." Marie says, still gasping for air.
"That was me when I discovered this yesterday. I wish you guys could be here with me." I say as I turn the camera back to my face.

"We wish that too." Thew says.

I crawl back out of the dark shoe room and into the bright magenta room.

"Your house is amazing." Addy says.

"Thank you. Sometimes, I still have trouble calling it home though." I confess.

"Your home will always be back here. We all know it." Thew says.

Addy and Marie nod in agreement. "I miss you guys." I shed a few tears before heading over to the lift. When I get back up to the main level, I set my phone down on a box and give them a twirl from my dress.

"You'll win it." Addy says.

"For sure." Marie adds.

"You got this Sadie. We'll be watching twenty-four seven." Thew says.

"After all, the show starts this Friday, right?" Addy asks.

"Correct. This Friday. Wait. This Friday?"

"Sadie it's all right. Just do what you normally do." Marie says to calm me down.

"That's what my aunt told me to do when I failed the audition. I can't do this." The anxiety rushes back to me.

"Sadie, it's all right. You've got this. Just believe in yourself. Think of us. Think of Thew." Addy says. Thew gives a soft smile.

"We have to get lunch now. Just sew and you'll do great." Marie says trying to wrap things up before I lose my cookies on camera.

"Yep. Lunch. See you soon. Bye." Addy says and hangs up. Last time they tried to comfort me like this, I did end up losing my cookies so they know the deal now.

"What's that about?" Thew asks.

"Long story." I respond.

"Thursday?" He asks.

"Sure."

"Tomorrow it is." he says, "Love you."
"Love you too." Then we both hang up.
Tomorrow is Thursday and then it's Friday. The show starts in two days! I need to pull myself together. I start hyper ventilating. I go back into my closet and select a blue tank top and a pair of exercise shorts to wear while I start unpacking boxes. Soon, I'll probably only be allowed to wear my own designs. When I get back to my room on the main level, I drop my dress in the dirty clothes bin and the bin sinks into the ground and I look in the open hole in the ground. There's a machine that has tons and tons of hangers hanging from a conveyor belt type of thing. A hanger attaches to my dress and it gets filed into the correct category of dresses. The laundry basket comes back up from under my floor and I head to the living room. "Wow, that's cool." I say to myself. Somehow, nothing surprises me anymore.
I grab my shopping bags and let everyone know I'm unpacking. Everyone agrees and starts unpacking their things too. I get back to my room and dump all eight of my shopping bags into the clothes bin for them to get filed into my closet. Next, I go back into the living room and grab the last two boxes with my name on it. I bring them back into my room and walk down the hall to my office. I go through a few drawers before I find my scissors. I walk back to my room and cut the tape on the remaining boxes that Peter hasn't ripped open already. I unpack the first one with all of the little trinkets Dad has collected for me since I was younger. I go over to the empty table in my room and start placing the trinkets in the same order they were placed in my old bedroom. After I finish up with my trinkets, I go to the boxes with my clothes in them.

I grab one box and dump it out into the dirty clothes bin. I put the empty box right next to my other empty one. I grab the next box and dump it into the dirty clothes bin once it returns. I then place that box inside of one of my other empty boxes, creating a small tower.

The next few boxes have things like my bedding and stuffed animals. After that, I start unloading the old pictures I had in my room. I go back into my office and grab a hammer and a few nails I found in one of my drawers. I get back to my room and start hanging up the photos on my one wall that's not made out of window. I'm fine hanging up all my photos for about fifteen minutes but then I stop at one. The same one I paused at back home. The one of me through the ages with family and friends. It makes loads of memories rush back to me. Happy ones, like the day I met Addy and Marie and the days I would fly around in Dad's arms. The photo on the bottom of the frame of me hanging on to Thew's back brings back great, but sad memories. Like the day that he was helping me pack up my things. And how I couldn't bear it and just fell into his arms. I start to fall myself in real life and no one is there to grab me. I fall onto the floor and stare up at the ceiling. I miss home. And laughing hour. And Thew. All of it. I love New York too, but home is where I feel, well, at home the most. Home has my friends there. My dad. And everything in between from school to Mason's Cakes. Life will never be the same since I've moved here.

I sit up after a long gaze at the ceiling and finally hang up the photo. I continue hanging up photos and when I finish, I move to the next box with a few of my books in it. The next two or three boxes have books in it too. I unload the books and stock my favorites up on the bookshelf in my room and the rest of the books on the bookshelves in my office.

I unpack a ton of boxes of random junk until I get to the boxes with my sewing stuff in them. I start carrying the boxes two at a time to my sewing room. When they're all in my sewing room, I start unpacking. I put my fabrics from home into an empty bin next to my new sewing machine. I find my basic sewing tools in the next box and put those into a drawer in my sewing table. My last box I brought into my sewing room has my old machine in it. *Where am I going to put this?* I think. I walk out of my sewing room and into a different elevator at the end of the hallway. I press the up button and it empties me out into another hallway that must be upstairs. I pause before I walk into the room where I hear my aunt's voice. She's talking to my mom.

"Sadie can do it. I know she can." I hear Aunt Kara say.

"Sadie's going to get to the first round and get voted off. You shouldn't get her hopes up, Kara." Mom says.

My heart drops from my chest to my feet.

"Sadie's going to get through. I know it. She'll make it to the final round. She's a great seamstress."

"She doesn't have a competitive attitude though. That's important. Have you seen some of the girls? They're way older than her. They're not going to keep the younger girls so it's more of a fair competition. They have more years of experience. Do you see what I mean? She won't make it. Especially since she's been under so much pressure recently."

"Don't tell her such a thing. She's got it. I know she'll get it."

"And also, why all the money for your house when I'm in desperate need of money. Not just me. My family." Mom yells and cries at the same time.

"You're feeling a lot of emotions right now. It's the breakup and jet lag mixing together. Not a good thing." Aunt Kara says.

I feel like it's the perfect time to walk into the room so I slam open the doors. They both turn to look at me in surprise.

"How long were you here?" My mom asks angrily.

"Long enough to hear you don't believe in me." I look her dead in the eye. "I've got this."

"There are a lot of kids, Sadie. Don't get your hopes up." My mom says.

"I need help getting another table for my sewing room if you wouldn't mind." I look at Aunt Kara.

"No problem." she says. "Get some sleep." She tells my mom. Once she exits the room, my mom turns to me.

"Sadie, there's a lot going on between the breakup and moving. Are you sure you want to add more pressure to yourself?"

"Yes. I'm sure. I'll get that prize money and we'll get our house back." I say,

"Sadie. Don't you love it here?"

"Of course. It's wonderful."

"We're not moving back home and that's the end of the story." Mom says. Mom is the nicest person in the world but she knows how to be strict if she needs to.

"Sorry. I'm still going to get that prize money though and get that house." At that, I exit the room and use the elevator to get back to the main level.

I find Aunt Kara in my sewing room setting up an identical table to the one that already holds my new sewing machine. When she finishes setting up my new table, I plug in my old sewing machine.

"Thank you."

"It was no problem."

"For everything. For taking us all in and for getting me back onto the show and for believing in me."

"Sadie, don't get emotional with me." Aunt Kara gives me a big squeeze. "I have one more surprise for you. I arranged to have a private teacher come to the set of the show each day so that you can focus on the competition and not have to worry about missing any class credits. I just know you are going to do amazing things." She gives me another squeeze and turns to walk out of my room.

After she leaves the room, I start sewing using some of my old fabrics instead of unpacking the rest of my boxes. I just sew using my brain and put all the emotions that I've had from today into it. Scared. Angry. Anxious. Happy. I mix it all in and sew another dress, the color of a mango-pineapple smoothie. Well, more of a slushy. Some parts of the dress are specifically a sunset orange while others are specifically a yellow or a mix of the two colors. It's a short dress that goes down to my knees, so not very long. It has one sleeve that goes down to my wrist with a cold shoulder while the other sleeve is completely cut off and hemmed to be like a tank top sleeve. The dress also has a little triangular hole where a necklace would land if I was wearing one. It's perfect. I dress up one of the mannequins in my dress and then head back to my room and start unpacking the rest of my boxes.

Chapter 16

I make it a game. Drop my necklaces in the clothes bin.
Put the stuffed animals on the bed. I make it a race
against myself. I'm running so fast around the room; I
almost collide straight into Mark when he walks into the
room. I stop my feet when I see him but they slide across
the white plank flooring. I keep sliding and sliding and I
finally stop about an inch away from Mark.
"Sorry." I give an innocent smile and shrug.
"What are you doing?" He asks.
"Racing myself." I answer.
He gives me a quizzical look. "Why, exactly?"
"Unpacking is boring." I sigh.
"Got it." He nods understandingly. "It's almost time for
bed. Tomorrow is your last day to sleep in."
"Already? I was finally starting to have fun." I joke.
"I'll let you know when it's time. Love you."
"Love you too. Goodnight."
Mark nods and walks straight to the other side of the
hallway and into his room with Peter. When he's all the
way inside his room, I close my door for no further
interruptions and start the race again. I zip around the
room running from place to place and putting things up
where they go. I'm finally down to the last box. Thank
goodness. I open it up and realize this wasn't a box I
packed, but something my friends packed. There is
confetti everywhere inside the box and on top of it sits a
yellow binder.

I pick it up gently and open it. As I flip through the pages, I realize that each page is a handwritten note from my friends from school. Somehow, Sonata was able to get a note in too. As I read through them, I start to get teary. Even the note from Brianna was heartfelt. I miss home so much and wish I could go back. Just for a single minute. To see Thew and Addy and Marie. I would give them all huge hugs and by the time I would be done hugging them, my time would be up and I'd be fine with that. Just to at least know that they're there. Not just a picture in my head.
I place the yellow binder on my desk, plug my phone in, and head to my closet. I slide down the fire pole and walk into the dress area. I see a night gown that I want to wear but it's on the top rack. How am I going to get twelve feet up there? I step on the bottom rack and reach for the next one but it's too far up so I fall backwards. This time, I get up onto the rack again and jump and reach the next rack. Yes. I'm too busy celebrating that I lose grip and fall backwards, again. Let's try this one more time. I grab onto the step and onto the rack once again and jump to the next one. This time, instead of celebrating, I hoist myself onto the next rack and stand on it. Easy. Just like climbing a tree, which I'm very good at. I repeat the steps over and over until I to the top rack and pull the night gown down. I look down to position my next move but that was a mistake. I start to feel dizzy and can't stand now. I look up and start yelling for help. I'm so high that if I reached my hand up, I could touch the twelve-foot-tall ceiling. I cry for help louder and louder until I finally lose my voice. Great. After a few minutes of hanging on for dear life, the robot for the house turns on.
"How can I assist, Sadie Benton?"
"Help." Is all I manage to get out.

"Unleashing ladder." Suddenly, a ladder flies out in front of my face and I grab onto it, putting the night gown in my mouth while I climb down. So much for a night gown. At least now I know there are ladders. Phew. "Thank you." I say to the robot.

"Anytime. Calling wardrobe." Now the wardrobe comes flying from the very back of the last room and lands directly at my feet. The doors fly open and I stare at them, not knowing what to do. The robot starts talking again. "All aboard." It says in its robotic voice. So, I do what I think is the only logical explanation for 'all aboard.' I hop into the wardrobe and sit crossed legged inside of it. Then, it zips off to the fire pole and I feel like I'm riding Hang Time. The wheels on the bottom of the wardrobe are magnetic and I'm heading straight upwards. Just straight up. Completely vertical. I grasp onto my stupid night gown that got me into this mess. When we finally make it to the top, the wardrobe starts moving, at what feels like fifty miles an hour, only to come to a halt about a foot from where it started. I crash out of the wardrobe landing face first into my floor. I wish I'd closed the doors. I stand up and take my clothes off to get changed into my night gown. When I finish, I put my old clothes into the clothes bin and walk straight up to bed. No one needs to tell me to go to bed. I get under the covers and fall fast asleep, leaving the light on and not even caring.

I sleep in the next morning having no such thing as school to worry about. When I wake up, I go into my closet, grab a shirt and shorts using the ladder this time, and get back up to the main level. I put the night gown in the dirties and get ready for the day.

I walk into the living room and turn on the TV to the FOTR channel to see who got into the show from the auditions last night. From what I can see, Tiny made it, the little girl from yesterday's auditions still got in, and the rest of the people who got in yesterday, plus a few more. In total, there's twelve people who are competing including me. That means, to win this, I'll have to beat eleven other people. One of which is my new friend. I take a deep breath in and a deep breath out to calm myself before my nerves get the better of me. I leave on the TV and stand up to go find my aunt. I walk around the house a bit and find her in the kitchen cooking pancakes.
"Good morning." She says happily.
"Good morning." I say and give a yawn.
"It's a big day tomorrow." She grins.
"Yep." I give another yawn. Why am I so tired?
"We're almost done unpacking the boxes already." Aunt Kara says, sensing my nerves and changing the subject.
"Already? It took days and tons of neighbors to get the house packed up."
"I know. Isn't it crazy?"
"Yeah. Tiny made it on to the show."
"Good for her. Aren't you excited?"
"Well, not really. I mean of course I am. It's just that I'm going to make a lot of friends on that show and I have to vote the design I don't like off. What if that's Tiny's?"
"I know sweetheart. The good thing is it's just a game. You can still be friends with them in real life." Aunt Kara says as she flips a pancake. "Wanna try?"
"No thanks." I answer. I know my situation isn't a big deal but I feel like it is. I don't want to hurt anyone's feelings. I walk out of the kitchen and into Mark and Peter's video game room where I hear them yelling at the screen.

I open the door. "Good morning, guys."
Peter lets out a bloodcurdling scream at the game and
Mark nudges his arm. "Oh. Hey there, Sadie." Peter
finally says and automatically gets back to his game.
"Do you want to play?" Mark asks kindly.
"I'm not much of a gamer but I'll try." I answer. Mark
gives me a controller and invites to play the game. It's
some sort of fighting game. "How do I do this?" I ask.
"This button is kick. This button is punch. This button is
flip and that one is jump." Mark explains pointing to each
different button on the controller.
"Why would you need to flip?" I ask curiously.
"So, you can land on someone's head and knock them
out." Peter answers quickly while still playing his game.
"You know we need to start the game over since Sadie is
joining and since I haven't been playing for the last three
minutes." Mark looks at Peter. "I don't know how my
character is still punching you."
"No. I'm punching your dude." Peter snaps back.
Mark clicks a button on his controller and it takes the
game to the main menu. I click the button on the top of
my controller to join the game and select my character. I
choose this super buff looking girl that's named Cassy.
Mark chooses this tall demi-god person and Peter chooses
a sumo wrestler guy. My character has no chance at
winning this. Mark presses play and our characters get
transported to a boxing ring. Big numbers appear on the
screen.
3,2,1, FIGHT.
I start spamming random buttons and knock out Peter
with all my kicks. He throws down his controller in anger
and crosses his arms around his chest.
"Whoops. Sorry." I say,

Then I start spamming the flip button and land directly on top of Mark's character and he gets knocked out too. Now huge words go up on the screen.

**PLAYER
THREE
WINS**

Confetti falls everywhere across the screen and my character pumps her fist in the air.

"That was a glitch. I win everything." Peter yells. "I demand a rematch." He clicks a few buttons on his controller and a new match begins. All that I do is exactly what I did last time. Spam buttons. This time I knock out Mark first and then Peter comes and tries to do a flip on top of me but I spam the kick and jump button and knock out Peter in midair.

"WHAT?" He screams.

"I'm actually pretty good at this." I smirk. This just makes Peter angrier. Aunt Kara comes into the room and lets us know that breakfast is ready so we all walk out of the room and sit down on the couch with our plate of pancakes.

"Thanks for breakfast." Mark tells Aunt Kara.

"Oh, it was nothing." Aunt Kara smiles happily.

I gobble down my pancakes in three minutes flat and stand up. "I think I might get some sewing in." I tell everyone.

"You're going to be sewing for a whole month straight starting tomorrow. There're so many other things to do." My aunt says. "It actually surprises me because she loves sewing more than anything in the whole world."

"I just, well, I want to practice for tomorrow if you know what I mean." I respond.

"You'll do fine." Peter grumbles. "Tomorrow, just sew like how you keep killing me on this game."

I run up to him and give him a hug. "I'll stay out of the gaming room from now on."

"Well, first I need to beat you." He stuffs the remaining bites of his pancake into his mouth and runs back into the gaming room. I follow him inside and grab my controller. I'll have time for sewing afterwards. He turns the game back to the main menu and chooses two players instead of three. "This time, I'm playing your girl."

"Fine." I say coolly. "I'll play your character."

"Deal." Peter selects Cassy and I select the sumo wrestler whose name is apparently XJ. Peter presses the start button.

3,2,1, FIGHT.

This time, I start spamming random buttons and kick Peter's character in the stomach. When I do, it pops out a gift and I collect it by walking on top of it. A huge star blows up the screen and XJ holds a bow and arrow. When Peter's character gets back up, I start spamming buttons again and the arrows get launched. One arrow that I shoot catches on fire and creates an explosion. This knocks out Peter's character and he drops his controller on the floor.

"How?" He says in awe.

"Now, I'm going to go sew." I say, like I'm in charge.

"Wait." Peter pleads.

"Yes?" I turn to look at Peter.

"I need to win at least one. Please?" Peter says desperately.

"Fine. I'll let you win this one." I agree.

"No. That's not right. I need to win with you really trying." He whines.

"Fine. I just really need to sew."

"You're going to be sewing all day tomorrow."

"I know. I know. I just want to practice." I press the play button on the controller and select Cassy again. I spam the buttons again and again and defeat Peter like twelve times.

"Just one more?" He asks.

"You said that like an hour ago. I need to practice. If I can't sew tomorrow, I can't win the prize money. Then, I become a failure in front of all of America and we can't get our old house back." I yell at Peter. I think I've had too many hours of video games today.

"Chill girl. You'll do fine. You've been sewing since you've walked. You've got this." he says, "You know, I want our old house back as much as you do." He adds.

"I thought you wanted to stay here forever." I say standing up.

"It is pretty great but I grew up in that house as did you and Mark." He says as he chews on his cheek making a plan to defeat me in the game.

"Fine. I'll do a couple more rounds with you. Then, I sew."

"Deal." He presses the play button and I spam the kick button until I get a fire bow and arrow from a temporary knock out. I shoot the arrows at Peter's character and I win the round. This happens over and over. Three 'o' clock. Four 'o' clock. Five 'o' clock. Five thirty.

Mom knocks on the door. "Dinner time."

"What?" Peter and I both say for different reasons.

"I never had time to sew." I complain.

"I was never able to beat her." Peter says getting frustrated.

"Sadie, you'll be sewing all day tomorrow. Peter, you can play your stupid video game any day." Mom says. "Time for dinner."

Peter and I both stand up and walk to the dining table in the middle of the living room. We both sit down on either side of Mark and slump down in our chairs. Mom sits down across from Peter as Aunt Kara comes into the living room with plates filled with pizza and bowls full of soup. Weird combination tonight but it works. I'll eat just about anything since I skipped lunch. Aunt Kara sits down at the chair across from me and leaves the chair in the middle empty.

"Who's that for?" I ask kindly.

"No one in particular." Aunt Kara answers. Then, she smiles and pats the chair and the little Dachshund named Queen jumps up on the chair.

"Where has she been?" I ask excitedly.

"She was at a pet hotel while we were getting everything moved in for you guys. She would have gotten lost in the maze of boxes." Aunt Kara giggled.

"But when? I've been at the house all day and haven't seen you leave." I say,

"You were playing your game with Peter. Mark came with me too."

"How did I not notice?" I ask no one in particular.

"I'm glad you guys have been enjoying your games." Aunt Kara says.

"I always win." Peter grins.

I roll my eyes. "You're so great at the fighting game." I say sarcastically. Everyone at the table starts laughing and we dig in to our dinner.

After we finish dinner, I change for bed and brush my teeth. Next, I walk into my sewing room and sit down at the table with my old machine. I grab one of my old fabrics and clip it onto my machine. I thread the needle and push my foot down on the pedal for a split second before Mom comes in.

"Time for bed, honey." She says kindly.

"What?" I protest. "It's like eight. I haven't had time to sew at *all*." I make sure to add extra emphasis to the word "all."

"Well, I'm sure you'll be tired of sewing by next Friday. Head on to bed now." she says,

I stomp out of my chair and flip the *on* switch to *off* angrily. I shove past Mom and slip into my room. I slam the door behind me. Instead of plugging my phone in, I bring it up to bed with me and text the group chat with Marie, Addy, and Thew.

Me: How've you guys been?

Marie responds immediately.

Marie: Great. You?

Me: Fine. I've been beating Peter in video games all day.

Addy: Sick.

Thew: I've never been good at games. LOL

Me: Me neither. Somehow, I keep crushing him. I played at least seventy-five rounds today.

Addy: What game?

Me: Some fighting game. Don't know what it's called.

Addy: I have all sorts of fighting games. Just name one.

Me: I don't pay attention to the names. Besides, we only played one game today.

Marie: What outfit did you wear today?

Me: Just something casual. I wasn't planning on going anywhere.

Addy: What are you wearing for the show tomorrow?

Thew: The green one would look nice.

Me: Then the green one it is.

Thew: :)

Addy: When are you starting school?

Me: My Aunt Kara hired a private teacher to work with me while I'm on the show so I can still get my class credits.

Addy: You are SO lucky.

Marie: : (I love school.
Thew: I don't mind it but I'd rather be on summer break.
Me: Always.
Thew: I have to eat dinner. Sorry to cut it short.
Addy: Me too.
Marie: Me three.
Me: All at the same time? LOL
Addy: All our families are having dinner together tonight.
Me: Fun. I'll let you guys go. I have to get to bed.
Goodnight.
Thew: Night.
Addy: See ya.
Marie: Goodnight.

I turn off my phone but can't help but feel sad. All three of their families getting together when I'm not there. I mean, New York is my home now but I can't help but feel a bit sad and alone. I close my eyes to shut the thoughts out of my head and soon fall asleep.

Chapter 17

I wake up at five with a sick stomach and bad thoughts from the nightmares I had. They weren't necessarily the nightmares an average kid my age would have. It's more about me being the first person to get voted off the show and just strange unrealistic dreams about Addy and Thew. None of my dreams are leaving me as I go to the bathroom and brush my teeth. I thought that five minutes after you wake up, you're not even supposed to remember your dreams. Apparently not. I brush my hair next and put it into a pony tail. I walk slowly out of the bathroom and I open the doors to my wardrobe and hop inside. It stops me right at the dress area so I hop out and use a ladder to get the short green dress that Thew wants me to wear today. I ride the wardrobe to the last room of my closet and hop out. I pull the hanger off of the rack and wait for the little door opens up so I can crawl through. I set the green dress neatly in the wardrobe and crawl into the shoe room to retrieve a pair of emerald heels. I walk a few feet down and grab the emerald heels. I walk back and crawl through the hole again. I think I'm getting the hang of this. I put back the hanger and the hole closes back up. I drop the emerald shoes into the wardrobe and plop myself into the wardrobe with my shoes and dress. I close the wardrobe doors over me and I feel the wardrobe take off on its tracks in my closet. My back presses right up to the back of the wardrobe and I feel the pressure of the wardrobe going straight back up into my room. It stops for a millisecond and starts going super fast only to make me crash against the doors of the wardrobe. Soon, I'll get the hang of that too. Right? I undress and drop the night gown into the dirty clothes bin.

I walk into the bathroom and set my dress and shoes down on the counter. I then turn on the shower and get in. At first, I just sit there letting the warm water run over my body. I let the thoughts whirl around in my head and then I empty them with the warm water that goes down the drain. Then, I get bathed and hop out of the shower. I take a deep breath to inhale the hot, humid, air around me. I slip on my green dress and put on my heels. I close the bathroom door to look at myself in the mirror that hangs on the back of the door. Beautiful. I brush my hair and put it in a high pony so it'll stay out of my face when I'm sewing. I brush my teeth and go back into my room. I crawl onto my bed and grab my phone from where I left it last night. I grab my phone and bring it back down to the ground with me and sit on my bean bag laid out on the floor. *I'm going to text Thew.* I think. *We haven't had time to talk alone lately.* For some reason, nothing comes to mind or feels like the right thing to say. So, hello is all I ended up saying. Somehow, he responds immediately.

Me: Hello.

Thew: It's two in the morning here.

Me: Whoops.

Thew: It's fine. My family just got back from the party at Addy's house. I'm lying-in bed so you didn't wake me up yet. LOL.

The pang of uncertainty hits me again.

Me: Did you have fun?

Thew: Sure did. Wish you were there too.

Me: It's a school night for you. You should have been in bed like three hours ago.

Thew: I think we might have to skip school or call in late today. I need sleep.

Me: LOL. You better get started then. I'll leave you alone. I'm bringing my phone with me to the filming so text me whenever you want.

Thew: Thanks for checking in. We haven't had a lot of time together lately. I'll call you later today. Goodnight.
Me: Night.

I turn off my phone and get out of the bean bag only to move a few feet across the room to the chair at my little desk under my bed. I sit in the chair and spin around and around in circles until I feel sick. I love these spinney office chairs. I pause for a second to set my phone down on my desk and keep spinning. I do this just to kill time until six when I'm really supposed to get up. I spin around and around and don't stop until Mom comes in.

"Time to go, sweetie. Bring your phone because Aunt Kara and I are dropping you off."

I keep spinning.

"Sadie. You're going to be late. You're supposed to be eating breakfast in the car so don't make yourself sick now."

Spin, spin, spin.

"Sadie Serra Benton. Get off that thing now." My mom says as she walks up to my chair and sets a hand on it so I can't spin anymore.

"I'm going to be stuck sitting around all day." I use as an excuse to spin. "Just let me use the spinney chair one more," I pause. "Ok. Your right. I'm feeling sick."

"Good. It's time to get in the car."

I hop out of the chair and walk around in a zig zag line for a bit until I crash into a wall. I think I woke up to early. Mom walks back to the desk and grabs my phone.

"Forgetting something?"

"Right." I take it from her and she snatches it right back.

"What?"

"Ten percent battery? Sadie, how can I contact you like this?"

"Whoops. Sorry." I take the phone out of her hand so she doesn't start looking through my text messages. I'm feeling playful today so I take off down the hall and run into the elevator that awaits me. The doors close with me inside the elevator and I press to go to the parking garage level. Mom rolls her eyes as I go down and wave at her. She waves back a little wave and I'm off down the elevator.

When I reach the garage level, the limo sits there waiting for me and Aunt Kara, Mark, and Peter all wave at me from the back. Ronald hops out of the car and opens the door for me.

"Thank you." I smile at Ronald. I hop in and Aunt Kara gives me my breakfast bag.

"Thanks, Aunt Kara." I look around the limo. Mark and Peter are wearing suits and Aunt Kara wears a fancy dress with a long cape sort of thing that goes out over her shoulder. It's beautiful. "You guys got dressed up."

"I can't tell you how many times Mom begged me to get this suit on." Peter exclaims.

I roll my eyes. "Your dress is great. Did you sew it?" I ask Aunt Kara.

"As a matter of fact, yes. I did. You really think it's great? It's a new design."

"It's not great, it's amazing."

"Oh, thank you." Aunt Kara says, flattered. "Now your mom left me in charge of you and how much you eat so you better get to it." She points to my bag. I stuff myself with freshly picked fruit and miniature pancakes that were all in the bag. By the time we get to the studio, I'm just about finished with my meal in a bag. We all get out of the car and Mark, Peter, and Aunt Kara follow me through the studio to the front desk where I check in for the show.

"Sadie Benton?" The lady at the front desk asks dully.

"Correct."

"Follow me." She says like a robot. She gets out of her chair and walks me to the hair and makeup department. "You start here. Follow the instructions from the staff in there from now on." She opens the door for me. I give Mark, Peter, and Aunt Kara a huge hug and they bid me good luck. I run happily into the door and sit at the vanity chair marked with my name. A lady runs up to me, much happier than the lady at the front desk.

"Hiya. Your're Sadie Benton?" I nod. "I'm your hair and makeup stylist. You can call me Carrie."

"Hey, Carrie." I wave.

"You can just sit here and I'll help make your hair stay up through the whole filming today."

I take a seat in the chair with my name on it and look at my reflection in the glowing mirror. Carrie takes out my hair tie and pulls out a brush. She brushes my hair till it's the softest it's ever been. She grabs one of her fancy hair ties and pulls my hair up into a high pony, but even higher and more stable. She stands back and spins my chair around. She doesn't even know how much I like spinney chairs.

"Nope." She says to herself. She spins me back around and takes out my hair, again. She brushes my hair in a completely different way than she did the first time. I didn't know there was more than one way to brush hair. She puts my hair in a high pony again, this time leaving me with long bangs on either side of my forehead. She spins me around to face her, once again. She tilts her head to the side. "Definitely not. Hmm." She puts her hand on her chin and you can tell she's thinking really hard. Suddenly, she snaps her fingers. "Got it."

She spins around and brushes my hair in *another new* way. When she finishes, she claps loudly and the other stylists turn around and start clapping too. "How do you like it?" She spins me around to face the mirror. The room suddenly goes silent awaiting my answer. I have one high pony, long bangs that are swept off to the side of my forehead, and two long strips of hair that dangle out of my pony tail on each side of my face. I like the way they shape my face.

"It's great." I say honestly.

The room erupts in thunderous applause.

"Thank you." I start to get out of my chair and Carrie steers my shoulders back into the chair.

"Not so fast. You still need makeup." She says excitedly.

"Oh. Right. Makeup."

"I'm thinking purple eye shadow to make a cute sort of match with your dress."

Carrie pulls out a huge compact of purple eyeshadow and gets a brush out of her apron. She dabs it inside the powder and brings the brush close to my face. I lean back more and more as the brush gets closer and closer to my face.

"What's the matter, little lady?"

"I don't do makeup." I confess. It's true. I don't do makeup yet.

"What? How old are you? Thirteen?"

"That's right."

"You're old enough to do makeup. All thirteen-year-olds use makeup." I shake my head. "Come on. A little won't hurt. You need some for the cameras anyway."

"Fine. Just the ones for the camera. No colors too if you wouldn't mind." I say,

"Why are you so afraid?" She asks.

"I don't have an urge to wear makeup and I don't want to start now. My mom is all about inner beauty."

"So, you're not allowed to wear makeup?" Carrie says with an understanding grin.

"Yes." I say sadly.

"Don't you worry. I'll only add the powder and blush for the cameras and some mascara."

"Mascara?" I ask, unsure.

"Trust me." Carrie says in her New York accent.

I close my eyes and she applies powder all over my face, something that's required when you're on camera, Carrie explains. She then adds some definition to my cheeks with some blush. Lastly, she adds some mascara to my eye lashes and when I open my eyes, I look like a completely different person. And I don't like it.

After I finish with the hair and makeup department, Carrie gives me a ticket that lets me skip through the costume department since I'm already wearing my green dress and I skip straight to the buffet. When I get in line, I get a plate of just fruit since I'm already stuffed from my breakfast in a bag. The people who helped me at the buffet were super nice too. They directed me to the door to the stage when I was done eating and I walked inside onto the same stage I did my audition on. It looks a little different now though. It has twelve lines on the ground marking the sections for the twelve different competitors. In the twelve sections, it has a small podium with a mic in the front of the section and a table with a sewing machine towards the back of the section. In the center of all the sections, a small circle sits in the middle. Inside each circle, sits two chairs and a glass coffee table in the middle of the two chairs. It has a red rose on one side of the coffee table and a stack of magazines on the other. In the middle of the two decorations on the table lay two handheld microphones. As I walk around the stage in awe, Brandon walks up to me wearing a bright blue suit with a purple tie. I almost didn't recognize him.

"How do you like it? I can show you your section if you want?"
"It's beautiful. And also, yes. I'd love to see my section."
"Great." He leads me over to a section that looks identical to all the others. "This is yours. Number six. Right in the middle."
"Wow. Thank you." I walk over to my sewing table and look at my bin of fabrics under the table. I start to walk over the red crack that divides my section from the two others on either side of me when Brandon starts yelling. "Don't step on the red line."
My foot stops in midair, literally three inches away from touching it. I pull my foot back to my section. "What's wrong?" I ask, suspiciously.
"This," Brandon pulls a remote out of one of his pockets and clicks a button. A huge, dimmed, glass divider shoots out of the red crack and I can clearly tell which space is mine. Brandon pushes another button and the dividers go back down into the cracks. "If you step on it, an alarm goes off and the dividers shoot out of the cracks." Brandon explains.
I run off the stage in fright.
"It's okay. As long as you don't step on them when the show's going on, you'll be fine. Have you gotten your mic hooked up yet?"
"No." I say.
"Alright. I'll lead you there."
 Brandon takes me out the backstage door and into the hallway. We walk into a door, right next to the hair and makeup department. "I'll leave you here." Brandon waves to a guy in the room wearing a black FOTR shirt.

He wears a set of navy-blue headphones around his neck. His jeans are completely black, with not a single hole in them. His shoes, well, those are another story. The man's shoes are just plain black tennis shoes that I saw at Mademoiselle Made for four-hundred-fifty-six dollars. He also has some black sunglasses that he wears, apparently indoors, that are so blacked out, you can't see his eyes. This guy must really make some good money here.

"I'm Rick." The man walks up to me and says. He shoots out his hand for me to shake.

"I'm Sadie. Sadie Benton." I shake his hand.

"Aww. The little girl with the fancy Aunt. Welcome. I'll get your mic on." He walks down the room and returns with a bright green microphone set. He clips the green battery pack on to the back of my dress and leads the cord up my neck and to my cheek so the actual mic rests just to the right of my mouth. He puts one piece of crystal-clear tape on my neck and another piece of clear tape on my cheek to hold the mic in place. He tucks the cord inside my dress so no one can see it when they're watching the show.

"Why is it green?" I ask.

"Oh. I forgot to mention, it's green because when people are watching your show," He starts.

I freeze him. "My show?"

"Well, you're in the show."

"Right. Go on." I prompt him.

"So, when people are watching the show, my buds here," He points to two people sitting at a computer. "They'll be able to easily spot the bright green microphone and edit it out so it looks like you're not wearing a mic when you actually are. Make sense?"

"Ohhh. Now I get it. I would've never thought."

"That's the point. The people watching won't be able to see it. I think you're all done in here. You should head backstage again because the show's going to start in a bit. You'll see the camera crew and the director will give you a script for the first few minutes of the show. Other than that, you can go off script and be more natural."

"Thank you." I run out the door and back into the stage room to go backstage and get my script. I can't wait for the show to start.

When I get backstage, the camera crew is setting up their cameras and rechanging batteries. When I walk in, they all wave at me. I wave back happily and walk over to the lady grabbing the director's chair from the closet.

"Hi." I say,

I guess I surprise the lady because she drops the chair.

"Whoa. You scared me for a second there." She picks back up the chair and looks at me. "You're Sadie Benton. Welcome. You look just like your aunt."

I laugh. "Thanks, I guess?"

The director laughs from behind us. "I've worked with your aunt on some TV shows she's been on. I've been waiting to see you get on something like this. I'm Aliya Griffinstone. I'm so excited to finally work with you after all these years of your aunt bragging about how amazing you are."

"Thank you. It's nice to meet you too. I'm here to pick up my script that a guy named Rick mentioned."

"Of course. You're getting straight down to business." Aliya gives me a sneaky smile. She walks over to another glowing mirror set up backstage and grabs a piece of paper. "Your script, my dear."

"Thank you." I grab it from her hand.

"You don't have to memorize everything. Just a brief summary of it." Aliya says. "Now, you go get started. We're on in an hour." She blows a whistle that hangs around her neck and she commands her staff to get things ready quickly. She grabs a rubber band and puts her light brown hair in a ponytail. She grabs her director's chair and walks out using the stage door.

I walk out the back door into a little garden behind the huge warehouse used as a studio. There are flowers beds everywhere and a huge circular fountain in the middle. Inside the fountain is a huge statue of Ashley holding a sewing needle that spits out a large stream of water. "They are going to have to get rid of that," I say out loud. Around the edges of the flower garden are little park benches. I sit down in one of them and watch the multicolored butterflies flutter happily around the garden. I pick up my script.

Act One, Scene One

Brandon sits in an interview chair while the first contestant walks up. They sit promptly in the chair opposite Brandon and Brandon fires questions at them. Brandon: Welcome to the show. We thank everyone for being here tonight. Please welcome our first and youngest contestant, Lucy Davis at age eleven. This goes on through all contestants;

1. *Lucy Davis (Age eleven)*
2. *Ivy Smith (Age thirteen)*
3. *Stella Wilson (Age thirteen)*
4. *Clara Campbell (Age fourteen)*
5. *Trinity Brown (Age fourteen)*
6. *Sadie Benton (Age twelve)*
7. *Chloe King (Age fourteen)*
8. *Alessandro Cipresso (Age thirteen)*
9. *Autumn Torres (Age fifteen)*
10. *Victoria Johnson (Age fifteen)*

11. Emily Garcia (Age fifteen)
12. Skylar Jones (Age sixteen)

Note to Brandon: Make sure to ask all contestants a mix of personal and fashion related questions; How did you start sewing? Who inspired you? Etc.
Note to contestants: You are organized in age groups. The number you are labeled with is what section you are assigned to. WARNING: DO NOT STEP ON THE RED LINES DIVIDING YOUR SECTIONS. Your lines are on the same pages as your sections.
I turn the script to page six and read on.
Brandon: Now tell me, when did you start sewing? Who inspired you? I know your aunt was a big part of this, am I right? How old were you when started sewing? Has your home always been in New York City? Tell me more about yourself.
Sadie: (Answer the questions honestly and in the exact order that Brandon reads them to you. Take the other microphone sitting on the table and speak loud and clear.)
I started sewing because _____.
When I was younger, I watched ______ that inspired me because_____.
My aunt was/was not a big part of this. She _________ and inspired me.
I was _____ when I started sewing.
Yes/No my home has always been in New York City.
More about myself? You're so kind. I _________.
(Fill in the blank spaces to tell the audience more about you.)
I stop reading when I get to the end of the page and start practicing my lines out loud. The door to backstage opens and Tiny and a smaller girl come running outside.

"Tiny."
"Sadie."
We embrace each other. It already feels like we're
best friends.
"Can you believe I got in?" Tiny yells.
"I can. And we're doing it together." I say excitedly,
feeling that an hour will go by fast.
"I know. Have you met Lucy? She's competing too. I
met her in the costume department. They gave me this
new hat to wear and a new pair of pants and a shirt to
wear on set. Oh. And these boots." Tiny says,
showing me her new cowboy hat, tassel pants, long
sleeve white blouse, and these shiny gold cowboy
boots that match with her hat. She looks fabulous.
"Wow. You look great." I turn to Lucy. "I'm Sadie.
You're Lucy, correct?"
"It's nice to meet you." Lucy shakes my hand
formally. But when she grabs my hand to shake, I feel
a literal electric buzz run through my body. Tiny and
Lucy both start cracking up so hard that I realize
Tiny's videotaping me. Lucy waves at me and shows
me the buzzer she had on her hand.
"Really? I'm going to get you back." I laugh too.
Tiny and Lucy sit down on the bench on either side of
me and Tiny shows me the video. I'm all happy and
then I look like a dog just bit me in the bottom. I
launch forward and my eyes practically bulge out of
my head. My hair goes static. "My hair. I'll have to
get it redone, you two." I say, poking Tiny on the
shoulder. Her white wavy hair bounces out around
her as she laughs. Then I start laughing too as all my
hair comes out of the pony tail. I don't really care
either. It looks fine either way. "Have you guys
gotten your scripts?"
They both show me their scripts.

"Right here." Tiny says, waving it around.

"I've got mine too." Says Lucy.

"You have to read your parts. Their kind of ridiculous." I laugh.

"You read my part?" Lucy jokes.

"No. Just mine. Mine's super goofy." I giggle.

We all go silent and look over our scripts until Tiny and Lucy start laughing hysterically.

"'*DO NOT STEP ON THE RED LINES DIVIDING YOUR SECTIONS.*'" Lucy mimics.

Tiny and I both laugh.

"I think we're all old enough to understand not to go into other people's sections." Tiny says.

The door to the backstage opens again and two more girls walk out into the garden. They see Tiny, Lucy, and I sitting on the bench and walk right over to us.

"You're Sadie Benton? A tall blonde girl says.

"Yes." I say confidently.

"You're Trinity? And you must be *little Lucy.*"

"Yes. I am Trinity and this is my friend, Lucy. Lucy Davis." Tiny says strongly.

"Whoa there. Slow down horsey." The tall blonde girl says in a very unnatural country accent. Tiny crosses her legs and arms and makes her best game face at the tall blonde girl. I have to admit, Tiny's pretty good at her game face. "I'm Skylar Jones. This is my friend Chloe King." The girl, apparently named Skylar, says in the regular voice that she used when she first asked who I was.

Just to be polite, I reach out my hand to both of them and shake it formally. "It's nice meeting you two." I try to say enthusiastically. I can tell their going to be trouble. When they walk to a bench farther down in the garden, I flip through some other pages in the script. The very last page is interesting.

You may now go off script for the rest of the show;
I think I have it down. I practice my lines over and
over again out loud and, in my head, filling in the
blanks as I go. I must have done it a hundred times
whenever a loud booming voice sounds out around
the studio, calling all contestants and Brandon
backstage. When I get backstage, Carrie comes
running over to me.
"Your hair." She pulls out a brush, curlers, and a hair
tie and leads me to a chair where I can sit while she
does my hair. Next, Rick comes over and tells me to
say something into my microphone. I try and nothing
happens. He presses a button on it and tells me to try
again. Carrie pulls on my hair while Rick tugs on my
microphone and suddenly, I feel stressed. I'm not
ready for this yet. The brush in my hair finally gets
through a knot that must have gotten itself tied in the
butterfly garden and my microphone gets peeled off
my cheek. Rick runs into the tech room. Carrie gets
my hair back up and is frantically styling my bangs
when Rick runs back in to give me another
microphone.
"Look up, Sadie." Carrie says in a stressed voice
while at the same time, trying to style my new bangs.
"Could you look a little down? I need to get this new
mic on. The old one was out of battery." Rick says in
a very rushed tone.

I move my head up for Carrie to style my bangs and when she finishes, I jerk my head down and Rick attaches the battery pack to my dress. He then tapes the actual mic and cord to my cheek and neck, just like last time.

"The mic was out of batteries and it was the same color as your dress so my buds couldn't find the mic on you when we were taping you in the garden. This one is more of a neon green than emerald." Rick explains. When he finishes, he rushes back into the tech room and comes back out with a little camera.

"Say something and look at me." Rick puts on his headphones.

"I'm Sadie?" I ask to the camera. I'm feeling really unsure about this whole show now. It's much more chaotic than I thought.

"Perfect. Mic is working and we can't even see it on you." Rick says taking off his headphones. "Don't touch it or jiggle it and you'll be fine."

"Got it." I try to say confidently. When Rick leaves, permanently back into the tech room, Carrie fusses over my makeup and reapplies my mascara, powder and blush.

"This time, I added a small bit of glitter under your eyes to make you stand out on camera." Carrie says excitedly.

"Thanks?"

"Of course. Now go get out there. Five minutes till showtime." Carrie rushes away and I'm left sitting at the chair with the glowing mirror desk that Aliya got my script from.

Five minutes go by in no time and I hear Aliya shout.

"Action."

Chapter 18

The word sends an electric shiver up my spine of fright
and giddiness.

"Hello, hello and welcome to the first episode of Fashion
on the Run: New York City." I hear Brandon start
talking. "Today, we have twelve contestants under the
age of seventeen that will be competing for one point five
million dollars. Let's bring em' out. Please welcome our
first and youngest contestant, Lucy Davis at age eleven."
Lucy skips out onto the stage, her brownish hair flowing
magically behind her. Her interview takes about five
minutes before she comes backstage again to join the
others.

"Now, let's bring our lucky thirteens out. Next up, Ivy
Smith."

A girl walks out onto the stage with dark black hair dyed
green on the edges. She wears a spiky jacket and ripped,
really ripped, dark black jeans. Her boots have spikes and
chains all over them and when she walks onto the stage
and takes her place, I can see she sits in the chair, legs
crossed, and blows a piece pink bubble gum. Thirteen?
How could her parents let her do that to herself? The
makeup, the piercings. Wow. Her interview lasts about
three minutes long before she comes backstage. I'm
guessing she's not a talker.

"Let's bring out the variety of the group, age fourteen.
Please welcome, Clara Campbell." I hear Brandon say.

A girl with long, dark brown hair, I guess must be Clara Campbell, walks out in a baby blue dress that's so long, it trails behind her like a wedding dress would. When she walks out of the curtains and takes her seat, there's still three feet of her dress backstage where I'm sitting. Her interview takes about six minutes before she comes back behind the curtains, tugging her dress to make it all fit backstage.

"Next up, from the one and only Lexington, Kentucky, Trinity Brown." Trinity does a little country dance out to the stage and plops down on the chair, with a flower stem in her mouth. Her interview lasts about five minutes, but I wish it was longer.

"Next up, the one and only niece of Miss Kara Calone, Sadie Benton. I hop out of my chair quickly and replay the lines on my script. I head for the curtains but stop for five seconds and think about all the good things in life that are waiting for me back home. Thew, my home, Addy and Marie, Ice with the Cream. The first step to all that is to get through this dang interview. I push the curtains aside me, feeling more confident than ever and do a casual catwalk down to my chair. I wave from side to side at the empty theatre chairs, pretending like there's people. I beam at the empty chairs and blow a kiss to the camera. It'll make for good TV, right? I sit in the chair opposite Brandon and cross my heels together looking and feeling like I run the world. I grab the microphone on the glass table and smile at Brandon.

"Welcome, Sadie. Are you excited for today?"

This wasn't on script but I know exactly how to answer that. "Of course. Who wouldn't be?"

Brandon laughs. "Now tell me, when did you start sewing?"

"Well, I started sewing when I was eight years old. I thought of it as a way to calm down and I really felt like I had a purpose."

"Who inspired you? I know your aunt was a big part of this, am I right?" Brandon prompts me.

"Well, you are correct. My aunt inspired me to start sewing and was a huge part in helping me get onto Fashion on the Run."

"Shall we watch a replay?" Brandon asks.

"Why not?" I reply. I know I've got this. On a huge screen behind us, it shows Ashley and Aunt Kara having their little argument about me. When the video finishes, Brandon starts talking again.

"Can you believe fashion idol, Kara Calone, thinks your great at sewing and Ashley doesn't?"

"Actually, I can." I reply with a wink.

"Tell us your story, would you? Has your home always been in New York City?"

"Well, my parents got divorced recently and my dad completely disappeared. I don't know where he went or have any clue why he left. After my mom and dad got divorced, my mom couldn't find work and couldn't pay for our house. So, we packed everything up and my Aunt Kara let us stay at her place."

"I'm so sorry. I truly am. Well, thank goodness your Aunt Kara is so generous."

I nod.

"Sewing is in your life for a reason, that's for sure. Well, we can't wait to see you in the competition."

I get out of my chair and wave to the fake audience and walk backstage.

The last few people go to their interviews while I wait backstage feeling like I'm on cloud nine.

When everyone else finishes their auditions, all the contestants walk out to their sections, careful not to step on the red lines. When we're securely inside of our sections, the dimmed glass dividers shoot up dividing the other contestants and I. The huge screen that replayed the scene with Aunt Kara and Ashley changes into a countdown.

5

4

3

2

1

 A huge buzzer sounds and I get straight to the sewing machine in my section. On the screen, a huge countdown of two hours and thirty minutes pops up and I hear the loud sounds of sewing machines and people digging through supplies. I get down on my knees and dig through my fabric bin. I find a beautiful purple silk fabric and grab a scissors I see laying on the top of my supply box. I do that weird thing where I have this pattern in my mind and my fingers just cut through the fabric, following the pattern in my mind. When I'm sewing, I feel like a different person where my hands just do whatever they want and my mind has no control over it.

I pin down the fabric in the way my hands want and notice the purple silk fabric turns out to be extra slippery, even with the pins. I add some more pins and put the fabric in the machine. I sit down and carefully, but quickly, sew through the fabric in a jagged, zig zag line. When I pull it out of the machine, my mind is telling my hands to trash it and start over again but my hands win the battle and I flip the fabric the other way so no one can see the seam I just sewed. I place the purple fabric that I just turned into a dress on the mannequin that sits to the right of my machine. I dig through the fabric bin again and find a fabric made entirely out of cork. I grab it and cut the cork to make straps for my dress. I pin the straps in the place that I want them and hand stitch them onto the purple silk. I go back to the fabric bin and find a beautiful fabric that has little roses on it. It looks kind of like a fish net but completely not. More of a lace, actually. I cut a diagonal line that goes straight through the middle of the fabric. I take the dress carefully off the mannequin and sew the beautiful lace onto the dress at the waist so it gives the dress the look of a salsa dancer. I look at the clock. Thirty minutes left. Has it really been that long? Time to kick it in high gear.

My brain tells my hands to go fast but my hands tell my brain to go faster. I speed down the section and practically crash into all the dividers. I dig through the fabric bin once more and find a little more of the purple silk and lace. I take them to the sewing machine and sew a little purple silk hat with the lace draping down the sides of it so it covers the face of whoever's wearing the hat with the beautiful lace fabric. I sew as quickly as I can to finish up the hat and when I finally do finish, I have exactly twenty-five seconds left to spare. I wipe the sweat off my forehead and tell my heart to calm down.

I see a camera giving the audience an overview of everyone working so I wave to the camera when it comes by me. I pin the hat onto the mannequin with my dress and stand back to make sure everything's finished. The timer buzzes and the dividers swoosh down back into the floor. A few workers come by and wheel our designs on the mannequins to another room.

"Please make your way to your podium." Brandon instructs.

I walk slowly to my podium and stand silently behind it. Am I going to get through the first day? I start to panic on the inside but remain calm, cool, and collected on the outside so I don't have a meltdown on camera. The screen changes from the countdown to a slideshow.

"Now, we will give you anonymous designs on the screen and after all twelve of them have been displayed, you will vote your least favorite off. After everyone has voted, the person whose design was eliminated will be permanently off the show. Are you ready to vote?" Brandon asks excitedly.

On cue, all the contestants shout, "Yes."

The slideshow turns on and plays through all the designs. A couple long dresses with frilly bows on the shoulder or on the waist. There're a couple fancy dress shirts, some for boys and some for girls. Then, there's my design. A purple, wrap around, dress that goes to about my knees. The little hat is what really tops it off though. Everything looks great. The slide show continues until the very last slide instructs the contestants to vote. My podium begins to glow and I look down at it. A screen appeared on it and it has photos of all the designs.

Click to vote out:

I scroll through and are about to click a dress that still has unsewn hems on it but pause. If I vote out all the easy losers now, I'll have big competition on the final rounds. I scroll back through the list and decide on a gold flapper dress that I think could win over mine in the future. After I click it, I step away from my podium to signal that I'm done. I look at the huge screen and see the number of votes in. So far, ten people have voted and we're waiting on two. A few more seconds go by and the final two votes are in.

"Now, wait one moment and I'll retrieve the envelope with the person being voted off." Brandon tells the other contestants and I. The backstage crew come back out wheeling the mannequins and placing them back in the designer's section. Next to me, I see Tiny sewed one of the dress shirts that's a beautiful shade of orange. Thank goodness I didn't vote her design off. I wave at Tiny and she waves back and then we both face back to center again. Brandon gets out of his chair and walks backstage. He walks back with the envelope neatly enclosed in his hand. Instead of sitting back down, he stands in the very center of the stage in front of the glass coffee table and slowly opens the card. Slowly. Very slowly. Sweat starts dripping down my face from the stress. I tuck my hands behind my back so I don't wipe the sweat off my face and draw attention to myself. It's me. I'm getting voted off. I just know it. My mom was right. I should've never done this. Now I'm not just a failure to the school but a failure to the whole entire United States. This is great. Just great.

"The first person to be eliminated from Fashion on the Run: New York is,"

Chapter 19

"Chloe King." Brandon says calmly, but with great suspense for the audience. The sweat immediately evaporates off my face and I feel a weight has been lifted off my shoulders. Phew. Episode one, completed.
"Commercial break. That's a wrap." Aliya announces.
I hop out of my section and run down the stairs. I can't believe I did it. I sit in one of the theatre chairs and one of the employees from backstage comes and serves everyone a glass of water as the other contestants come and sit down in the chairs next to me. Carrie and the other makeup artists come out next and reapply makeup.
"You did it." Carrie exclaims.
"I know. I thought I was toast." I admit.
"Your design was great. Never doubt yourself on those things." She wipes the makeup off my face and reapplies all of it over again so it looks new and fresh.
"Going back on in exactly one minute." Aliya announces.
"You better get going." Carries pushes me off the chair and I hop back into my section, as does everyone else except Chloe. She sits in the chair next to Brandon and her mannequin gets wheeled up behind the coffee table.
"We're on in three, two, one." Aliya shouts.
"Now tell me, were you surprised when you got voted off?" Brandon jumps straight down to business.
"Well, of course. Why wouldn't I be upset? MY design was the best out of all you fools'." Chloe crosses her arms and her high, blonde, bun flops on her head.
"So, why did you come here in the beginning? For the money?" Brandon asks curiously.

"Well, of course." I'm guessing that's her favorite phrase. "The money and fame means I become rich and famous. It's a simple equation. TV plus prize money equals fame and fortune." Chole bursts out.

"Well, let's take a closer look at the design you've created." Brandon waves his arm over her design as Chloe crosses her arms. "It's a magnificent piece, Chloe. How did you ever come up with that?" Brandon asks, trying to sound amused for the cameras and Chloe. Her design is quite magnificent. It's not the exact one I voted out but something like it. It's also gold but it has a huge bow in the center of it that's a ruby red color. I don't really think the two fabrics matched, so I think that's why she got voted out. Skylar must be upset.

"It looks like a dress I saw on a fashion magazine." Chloe grumbles with her arms still crossed.

"Beautiful. Was it the exact color combination?" Brandon says as he makes a crooked face at the color combination.

"Oh, shut up. I know it's bad." Chloe stomps out of the chair and pushes her mannequin over. The cameras tape her walking all the way across the theatre and slamming the exit door behind her, knocking over a water cup on the way. When the cameras focus on Brandon and the eleven remaining contestants, Brandon calls Skylar over.

"Welcome. Are you happy you made it through the first day?" Brandon asks, kind of changing the subject.

"Yes. I'm so happy." Skylar says sounding way happier than she was in the garden.

Is it because she made it through the first day or because she's on camera? I wonder.

"I have some clips of you in the garden with Chloe. Tell me, when did you guys become friends? Do you both live in the same town?" Brandon asks, as the screens play the clips of her and Chloe in the garden.

"Well, we both live in Southern California. I think we were on the same soccer team one year but we became fast friends earlier today." Skylar answers.
"Ah. I see. Well, I think you'll make a bunch more fast-friends because the remaining eleven contestants get a surprise party. Now you contestants, get on backstage and celebrate." Brandon says as he turns to us. He looks back at the camera. "I think that's it for today. Thank you so much for watching and make sure to join us next week for Fashion on the Run: New York." Brandon waves to the camera and so does the other contestants and I.
"That's another wrap." Aliya announces happily. She grabs her own cup of water and heads backstage with the rest of us for the party. We walk down a few doors to a room I haven't been in yet. When we stop at the door, she has the eleven remaining contestants grab the handle and push the door open. When the door flies open, I look inside and see a huge dance floor, similar to the one Gerta and I made back home. I walk inside with the rest of the contestants and I head over to a comfy-looking booth at the other side of the room. There's little I-Pads on all the tables that are showing replays of the episode. I sit down in a booth and a waiter comes up to me.
"What can I get started?" He asks kindly.
"Oh. Wow. It's a full-service night club." I joke.
"Sure is." The man laughs.
"I'll just get a cup of water, please." I say,
"Sure thing." The waiter rushes off into what must be the little kitchen in the backroom and leaves me to myself.
I only have a few minutes of me time because the boy contestant, Alessandro Cipresso, comes and sits in the other side of the booth across from me, having only the table between us.
He sits there for a minute just staring at me. What's his issue? "Can I help you?" I ask him.

"Oh, no. Just coming to have a little conversation. You wouldn't mind, am I right?" Alessandro gives me his best charming smile but fails dramatically.

"Sure." It's better to make friends than enemies in this game, right?

"So, your design was great. Where did you get the idea?" Alessandro asks suddenly.

"Um. I don't know. It just, came to me." I say nicely but a little stern. I don't like the feeling of this.

"Ah. I see. Where do you live?"

"Um. Up there." I point vaguely to the left corner of the room to signify that I live somewhere around here.

"Mhm." He nods. "Have you made any alliances?" He asks.

"Why are you asking?" I snap back. I'm really getting a bad feeling.

"Just wondering. You know, you can trust me." Alessandro gives another stupid smile.

"Right." I nod and try to smile back. Then Skylar walks up.

"Surprised you made it through the first day." She laughs at me.

"Yeah. Same with you." I say back. I feel utterly surrounded by the feeling that something bad is going to happen.

"You voted out Chloe. Didn't you? She actually got in with an audition. Your aunt just came and stomped on grounds to get you in. You don't even belong here. We're the professionals with real talent. You're just, the girl who has a famous Aunt." Skylar says raising her voice.

"Well, it's been a pleasure talking to you. Both of you." I nod at both of them and smile. I dash out the room. My makeup is sticking to my face, I feel it. I pull out my phone. I click on Mom's contact and click call. It rings. And rings. And then buzzes. I pull my phone down from my ear and look at the screen.

Low battery: 1%

Shoot. I lean against the wall. I miss home. I got through the first day. Yay. Until Skylar makes the point clear that I'm not supposed to be here. Then before that, some random guy who thinks he's so charming is trying to make an alliance with me? The day was going fine until it just flipped when I entered the disco room. Now I realize what it's from. I have no true friends here to celebrate it with me. Tiny is a great friend but Addy, Marie, Thew? I miss them. I feel the makeup melting more on my face. I get lost in my thoughts. Very, very, very deep thoughts. SLAM. Alessandro comes and leans on the wall next to me.

"What do you want? This isn't a good time." I grumble.

"One more question?"

"Fine. Yes?" I need to get this makeup off my face so I stop feeling so dirty. Then, I need to get home, plug my phone in, and call my real friends.

"So, no alliance?" Alessandro asks with a twinkle in his eye.

"Why? Why do you want it so bad? An alliance with me? I've barely even met you. How do we even make and alliance? We're separated by dividers. Glass dividers." I take out all my emotions on him and I kind of feel sorry for him.

"Wow. I like you. Are you single?"

I storm off down the hall. I've had enough of being cooped up here. It's only been a few hours but I miss home so badly. My real home. This is also only my fifth day in New York. I hear Alessandro running after me so I keep running down the hall, phone grasped in my hand. Or at least, I think. As I'm making a sharp turn to the exit, my phone slips out of my hand and lands face first, onto the marble floor. A shattering sound echoes through the empty hall as well as Alessandro' footsteps. When, he catches up to me, I'm staring down at my phone. He runs up to it and picks it up carefully.

"Oh. This isn't good." He whispers.

"What?" I grab it from his hand and stare at the cracked screen. "No." I cry. I hold it in my hand much harder than I was before and run out the door. Alessandro leaves me outside and I see him walk back down the hall through the glass doors. I stare down at my phone. The black, cracked screen. I hear the sound repeating over and over in my head. The crash on the floor. The impact of the glass hitting marble. Then, the treacherous sound of the glass cracking. I take a few deep breaths. *You made it through the first day. You wore makeup for the first time. Your family's going to be so proud of you. You've got this. You're coming back tomorrow for the second episode and you'll crush it again. Go tell the lady at the front to call Aunt Kara and all will be well.*

I listen to the tiny Sadie voices in my head and walk inside to the front desk. "I'd like to leave. Will you call my aunt Kara?"

The lady at the front desk looks up at me then down at her binder full of phone numbers. She reaches over to her fancy antique phone and carefully dials my aunt's number. After thirty seconds, the lady puts the phone down and points outside. She turns back to whatever she was doing before and I rush back outside. *You know what? I am doing fine. I was just feeling upset because I was stressed out that I wouldn't make it through today. I'll make the alliance with Alessandro and all will be well.*

And that's exactly what I tell Aunt Kara when her limo pulls up.

"You know, now that I think about it, the first show I was ever on was when I was fourteen too. I remember, I had the same freak out after the show was over too. It must be a stress thing." My aunt says kind of to herself and kind of to me.

"And you're not angry about my phone?" I ask carefully. I pass her the broken phone.

"Well, *I'm* not angry but this is for your mother to deal with. You'll have to show her when we get back to the apartment." My aunt hands the phone back to me and I take it carefully. I stare into the dark black screen. Wait. It's not completely black. I look deeper into it.

Someone's calling me. Thew? Wait, no. Dad? I jump in my seat.

"Dad's calling me." I bounce. "I need a phone charger, quick."

My aunt jumps too with the sudden amount of yelling and frantically searches for a phone charger. She finally finds one and hands it to me. I plug my phone in and click the "accept" button.

"Dad?"

Chapter 20

"Sadie? It's Dad." The phone answers. My hands start shaking with, what? Anger? Sadness? A tug of loss? "Where are you? Are you okay? How could you leave us?" I scream and cry into the phone all at once.

"I'm okay, Sadie. I just wanted to call to see if you're doing all right." He answers calmly.

"What? You *left* us. We're not doing fine. Why did you leave us? *Where are you?*" I explode with again, mixed emotions.

"You can't tell your mom or aunt about this, got it?" He says seriously.

"Ok." I say, even though it's on speaker with my aunt right there. "So, where are you?" I ask again.

"Sadie, it's for my job. They've called me to work and I had to leave all of a sudden." He explains.

"Mom says your cheating." I whisper agitatedly.

"Well, I can't answer anything about that." He whispers back.

"So, you are?" I ask with a fierceness in my voice.

"Sadie, I'm asking you to keep this private please. It was hard for me too, the last few weeks without my girl. I love you."

"I love you too." I whisper sadly back to him. I hear a big buzz that signals the end of the call and I put my phone down.

"He called you." My aunt says with happiness and anger at the same time.

"He misses me." I say sadly. "Maybe he'll call more often and it'll be just like Mom got a normal divorce? Not that divorces are ever *normal.*"

Then, the rest of the ride back to the apartment is silent.

I won't tell Mom about this but I'll tell Mark and Peter. I decide silently. When Ronald pulls up to the apartment and drops us off at the elevator, Aunt Kara and I hop in and the elevator speeds up to the top floor. Aunt Kara's little robot security system scans the two of us and lets us inside the penthouse. When I walk inside, it's completely silent with no sign of human life. I walk a few more steps inside the apartment and get an eerie feeling. *Where is everyone?*

"Surprise." Mark, Peter, and Mom all scream at the same time and pop out from under the couch and behind the elevator. They spray confetti poppers and throw Pop It's on the ground and all over Aunt Kara and I. I set my phone down on the coffee table and decide the rest of today is going to be a good day. Mark, Peter, and Mom keep throwing poppers and shooting confetti out of little cannons for a long time. Aunt Kara and I join and we destroy the whole entire living room. It's covered in confetti and the little wrappers of the Pop It's we threw.

"Thanks so much, guys." I tell them when everything runs out.

"Congratulations, Sadie." I hear three new voices coming from the TV. I look at the confetti covered TV and see a video call being projected onto the TV. I'm able to make out the faces of Addy, Marie, and Thew wearing little party hats. I run straight up to the TV and wave at them.

"Sadie, your shoes are *amazing.*" Marie squeals.

"The dress that you sewed was just the right amount of casual and fancy that the other contestants didn't see you as a threat or as a loser." Addy tells me.

"The hat was pretty cool too." Thew tells me.

"Thank you, guys. Aren't you supposed to be at school?" I laugh.

"Eh. We're all not feeling the best anyway from last night. Also, like half of the school missed today because they were watching your show." Addy explains.
"Really?" I say in exasperation.
"Yep. Also, you look really good in the green dress." Thew answers. "It matches your eyes."
"True." Addy adds.
"It's so beautiful." Marie squeals again. I reach up to the wall mounted TV and shove off some confetti so I can see them better.
"You guys all knew about this?" I exclaim. "I was talking to you guys and you didn't say a word last night." I laugh again.
"That was part of the plan." Thew laughs.
I sit down on the couch facing the TV. "You guys are funny."
"That's why you love us." Addy says.
Then, all of us laugh and just talk casually about life. Brianna is still acting like a freak and Mrs. Bronze still tries to boss people around.
"Oh. And guess what?" Addy says suddenly. "I got the DJ job for the dance."
"What?" I say excitedly. "You did it." I look across the ground for a minute and find an un-popped popper. I pick it up and throw it on the floor right in front of me. It makes a loud popping sound and Marie, Addy, and Thew laugh. "That's so exciting."
"Thanks." Addy giggles. "Marie is in the planning committee and Matthew just helps with decorations."
"That sounds so lame." Thew says to Addy.
I laugh. "I wish I could be there."
"We all do." Marie says.

We continue to just talk about life and spend the whole rest of the day talking. Mark and Peter pop in at one point to say hi to Addy's older brother and Mom pops in to say hi to Thew's dad. When it's far past ten 'o' clock in New York, I let them know I should get going. We all say bye and they wish me luck for tomorrow. When the call ends, I walk up to Mark and Peter.

"Do you guys want to come into my closet with me?" I say casually but with a sense of urgency in my eyes. I think they get the gist.

"I call dibs on the fire pole first." Peter yells and runs straight to my room. Mark and I follow him into my room and I pull on the dresser doors.

"Meet you slowpokes down there." I hop into the dresser as it flies down the pole with me inside of it. It wooshes all the way back to the last room in my closet and I hop out. I wait a few more minutes before Mark and Peter show up out of air from running.

"I call dibs on that thing next." Peter says as he puts his hands on his knees to catch his breath.

"What's wrong, Sadie?" Mark asks cautiously.

"Dad." I answer.

Peter pops his head up. "Dad?"

"He said not to tell anyone-" I start.

"You talked to him?" Mark and Peter say at the same time.

"Well, he called me in the car on the way back from FOTR. He told me not to tell anyone but he said he misses me. And yes, he is cheating, I think." I explain.

"He called you?" Peter is breathing heavily but I don't think it's because of how hard he was running.

"Yes. I don't know what to think of it. Or what to tell Mom." I confess.

"But why did Dad call you and not Mark or I?" Peter exclaims. "We were his first-born children. Not you."

"I know. And I don't know why he called me. I'm sorry.
I really don't know what to say."

"Well, you should. He called you and you're the special
one." Peter says mockingly.

"It's okay. We're always there for you. I'm glad you
came to us first." Mark explains, giving Peter a sideways
glance. "How about I explain it to Mom and save you the
trouble."

"Thanks." My shoulders sag in relief. "I really truly am
sorry. I don't know what made him call me or why.
Although, there is one thing I can say: race you to the
dress room." I automatically feel better and hop into the
wardrobe and close the doors. It speeds off heading out of
my closet but stops me at my dress room. That security
robot really is smart. I climb the clothing racks, just to
show off and grab a nightgown hanging on the very top
rack. I sit down on top of the very top rack and wait for
Mark and Peter. A race against his siblings is one thing
Peter can never resist. When Mark and Peter get into the
dress room, I laugh. Their reactions are priceless. Mark
gasps and warns me to be careful and Peter just grabs
hold of a dress and hoists himself up to the top rack
where I'm perched. He sits down next to me and does a
sort of monkey call that echoes throughout the whole
closet. Peter and I start laughing and keep doing a sort of
monkey call and hear it echo. I knew this would work.
After five minutes of this, Mark stands up.

"One of you is going to fall." He says seriously.

"Come gettttt usssss." Peter calls.

"Peter." Mark gives him a serious look. "Really?"

"Sorrrryyyy," Peter calls out again with a smirk. "That
you don't have amazing climbing skills like yours truly."

For some reason this annoys Mark more than anything else and he grabs onto a dress and hoists himself up as well. "You're coming with me." He grabs me by waist and takes a long dress that's hanging on the top rack. He grabs it with the hanger still on the dress and does a sort of lasso move. The dress twirls out of his hand and the hanger gets stuck on the chandelier above us. "Ready?" "Always." I answer. Mark has been wanting to get a job at the military after he finishes high school for the longest time, so he always has the coolest, yet safer, tricks. He holds onto my waist tighter with one hand and tightly wraps the dress in his other. He squats on the top rack and pushes off with his feet and we glide through the air. I feel like an acrobat in the circus. When the dress stops swinging from the chandelier, he slides down it gracefully with me still in his arm. When we reach the ground, he sets me gently back on the floor and unhooks the dress from the chandelier.

"See ya, Peter." He walks up to the fire pole and pulls himself all the way up the pole. I get into the wardrobe again and it brings me back up to the regular floor level where Mark is waiting for me.

"How is Peter going to get back up?" I ask Mark as I carefully get out of the wardrobe.

"He'll find a way." Mark shrugs.

"I thought you were the careful, cautious person."

"Ah-hem." He points behind me at the dirty clothes bin and I turn around. Sitting inside the clothes bin is Peter, holding on to a hanger for dear life.

"Epic." Is all Peter whispers. I walk right up to the clothes bin and pull him out.

"You found a way back up." I announce.

"Sure did." He dusts off his pants and shakes his hair out. "Now you better get to bed, Sadie. Another big day tomorrow." Mark tells me.

"I know. Love you guys."
"Love you too." They both answer as they shove each other out of my room.
I drop my green dress into the clothes bin and change into the nightgown, which as a matter of fact, is also green. I walk into the bathroom and wash my face to get rid of all the makeup and glittery stars on my face. I take out my hair as well and brush it a tiny bit more just to get rid of my bangs. I walk back into my room and check the time. I must have been at FOTR for much longer than I thought. I grab my laptop I haven't used yet and unplug it. I take it a few feet across my room and sit down in front of the huge window in my room that overlooks the city. It's beautiful at night. It looks just like the first night I got here. Not knowing if I would get onto the show or even if I'd survive without my friends here. I stare off into the distance at the Empire State Building with its little blinking red light at the tippy top. I look at all the huge buildings that make up all of New York City. I see all the little shops that Aunt Kara and I went to a few days ago and I see a few more apartment complexes that reach to the sky. I open my laptop.

Welcome, Sadie Benton. Have you used a laptop before? If so, click "Skip tutorial."

I click the skip tutorial button and it leaves me free to explore. I open my contacts and see all my contacts from my phone already uploaded to the laptop. I close out of my contacts and log into YouTube. I search up Fashion on the Run: New York.

The first video that pops up, posted by the official FOTR channel, has 3.5K views already. I click on the video and watch through the interviews. When my interview pops up, I watch through it intriguingly to see how I did. To me, I nailed it. My model walk was perfect and the way they showed Aunt Kara in the background was also perfect. I think I made a big impact. The video is only an hour long, thirty minutes of interviewing and thirty minutes of sewing. I think they had to shorten it because not many people would stay tuned for three hours of FOTR. When they show the sewing snippets, I realize that the microphone really isn't visible on camera. I watch through the whole hour of the first episode and scroll through the comments.

THEGRIM: Ivy's style is the best.

GLAMQUEEN: Chloe. You are my favorite and will always be. : (

LET'SDOTHIS: Sadie doesn't deserve to be on this show. Did you see her aunt? She bought her way into this. If she wins, I'll hate life. #BOOSADIEBENTON

MOI: I'm changing my name to that hashtag. My picture too. Have you seen the ridiculous photo of Sadie while she's sewing? I'll send you the link, #LET'SDOTHIS: www.https//SADIEBENTONTHEAWKWARD

LET'SDOTHIS: Thanks, MOI. Love the pic.

As I read through the rest of the comments, nothing gets better. I click on the links and see me making weird faces on the show. I look like a jerk when I sew. I scroll through the hundreds of comments about how amazing the other contestants are and how everyone hates me. It takes everything I have not to respond with some dirty thing to those people myself. Instead of sadness overwhelming me, I'm filled with fire. They don't know who I am. I'll show them. Tomorrow is the special episode because it's two days in a row instead of weekly. Everyone will be watching that. I look off of the screen and out at the blinking red light on top of the Empire State Building. I'll show those people who I really am.

Chapter 21

The next morning comes in a breeze. I slept like a baby last night as I was planning my master plan. I get up and get dressed in a flashy gold dress that goes down to my knees. I throw on some knee-high, sparkly, gold, heel boots to match. When I get inside the kitchen, I sit down and shovel my favorite blueberry pancakes Aunt Kara made me into my mouth.

"Let's go." I order after I'm finished.

"Whoa. Who's in a rush today? Were you late yesterday?" Aunt Kara asks as she cleans up dishes.

"No. Just want to get there. Alessandro is waiting." I say, "And so is my master plan." I whisper to myself. I feel like a spy on a mission. An animal ready to attack its prey. Silent, but deadly. I jump in the elevator and it whisks Aunt Kara and I down to the main level. Ronald already awaits us and I hop into the car. He speeds down the road and comes to a halt at the studio. Aunt Kara moves to get out with me.

"Would you mind staying in the car today?" I ask as politely as I can.

"Oh. Well, okay. Are you feeling alright?" Aunt Kara asks suspiciously.

"Fine." I take a deep breath and give her a thumbs up. Ronald closes the door and I rush into the studio. I zip around corners and don't even wait for the dull lady at the front desk to escort me. I run straight into the hair and makeup department and sit in my chair. Carrie rushes over to me instantly.

"Well, you're here early. For today, I'm thinking some cute pigtails with a little bow in the corner. You see where I'm going? It's day two so day double?" Carrie nudges me. "*Two* pigtails?" She frowns. "No?"

"I was thinking more of a cool hair style. One that really makes an impression. I also need some bold makeup that makes me really stand out against the crowd. Have any ideas?" I explain.

"So, you're fine with wearing a lot of makeup? Like, a lot a lot?" Carrie asks with a face no one can read.

"Yes." I say confidently.

"I thought you'd never ask." Carrie beams and gets to work immediately. She grabs some hair dye and some glitter and flushes it into my hair gently.

"I'm going to need you to lean back for this one." Carrie pushes a button that makes my chair recline into a warm pool of water that wasn't there a second ago. She grabs a small comb out of her apron pocket and combs some smooth substance into my hair while it's bathing in the pool of warm water. I close my eyes and feel the warm water soak into my scalp. It feels like a warm hug from the person you love the most. It soothes all my problems as it flows gently through my hair. People will love me. They'll have no choice. I'll be the star of the show today. After all, it *is* double day so double the luck for me. I drift off for a few minutes as Carrie works with my hair in the warm bath of water.

When I wake up, my chair has been lifted back up to its normal seated position. She styles and curls and straightens. It makes no sense in my mind. Once she's done with the style of my hair, she adds small details to my hair. Then Carrie starts working on my makeup. I can't help but stare at myself in the mirror. I like it a lot, but it's different. My long black hair has been styled into a bob where one side of my hair hangs a little bit over one of my eyes. It has golden streaks every two inches all the way around my hair. There's also a small tad of gold glitter lightly sprinkled around my hair. Then it strikes me.

"Did you use a scissors?" I start to panic. My long hair took a long time to grow.

"A scissors? Oh. Why never. That hair must have taken a long time to grow out." Carrie exclaims.

"Thank goodness." I sigh in relief. When Carrie finishes with my makeup, a dark blue and green eye shadow with a glittery gold eyeliner, a bright red lipstick, and a glittery gold rose on my cheek, I thank Carrie so much, I think her mind might explode.

"It's perfect. It's exactly what I was looking for. Thank you. Thank you, thank you, thank you." I exclaim with happiness.

"Oh, it was no big deal." Carrie says modestly. "Just head up the staircase to the right and walk down the hall three doors."

"Thank you." I yell. Then I run out the door and stop a few feet outside the door. I pop my head back through the door. "Thanks." Carrie waves and shoos me off to the costume department where she says they have something I might want. I rush right across the hall and up the staircase to pause at a door with a huge star on it.

Costume Department. It reads. I swing the door open with excitement and fire and prance right in. Nothing's going to stop my day. Except, the only person who might, Skylar.

"What are you doing here?" She snaps.

"Um. Looking at clothes." I say back.

"That's your casual wear? Why do you even need the money? You're already so rich. People like Tiny need the money to actually own a house, not a barn." Skylar says angrily.

"How do you know about that?" I ask suddenly.

"You're not the only with a *tiny* ally here." She snaps again.

The lady who must work at the costume department comes back into the costume room. "Ladies. If we cannot co-exist, one of you will be removed."

"I was here first." Skylar yells.

"You sound like you're in kindergarten." I yell at her.

"Both of you. Stop. One of you is Sadie?" The costume department lady asks us nicely.

"That would be me." I walk up slowly to the costume department lady.

"Very well. The other one of you, grab what you're looking for and get out. There's no trouble here in my department." The lady says angrily. "And make it snappy."

Skylar hops off of the small carpeted stair she was standing on, most likely waiting to be measured for something, and stomps off to the door, scratching her sharp nail against my rose. I put my hand to my cheek.

"You're Sadie?" The lady asks, clarifying.

"Yes mam." I say as I take my hand off of my cheek.

"Good. I have your reserved jacket from Carrie." The lady whisks through the hundreds of clothes racks knowing right where she's going and returns holding a short, black, leather jacket.

"Whoa. Thank you." I say as I take it delicately from her hands.

"You can try things on up there." The lady points to the small carpeted stair where Skylar was standing.

Although, when I step onto the stair, I notice there is a huge window wall that overlooks the main stage. I take another step up and then to the next step and onto the big, circular, carpet area that overlooks the main stage below us.

"I didn't know we were this far up." I gasp.

"Yes. Quite beautiful." The lady responds.

"Earlier, you said in *your* department. Do you own the costumes here?" I ask the lady. She seems a little lonely.
"Well, I sewed all of these." The lady opens her arm to indicate all the hundreds of clothes racks in the room.
"Wow. All of these?"
"Of course. Sewing is my passion." The lady walks out of the wall of clothing racks and points at my jacket. "Try it on, will you?" She urges.
I gently take the hanger off the jacket and slip it on. The lady comes up and tightens a few buckles around my wrist and shoulders.
"Perfect."
"Whoa." I spin around to admire the jacket. "Thank you, um,"
"Ying." The lady answers as she tightens her black bun in her hair.
"Yes. Thank you, Ying."
"Now, shoo shoo. I have some work to get done." Ying disappears into the wall of clothes racks again and I exit the room.
When, I look in the mirror on the back of the door to the hair and makeup department, I realize that the scratch on my rose makes me look majestic so I decide not to go to back into the hair and makeup room. I walk out onto the stage and walk-up onto Alessandro' section where he sits, staring at the sewing machine.
"Hello." I say nicely. He jumps an inch off his chair and turns around.
"Oh. You. Hello." He dusts off his shirt and sits straighter up in his chair.

"I just came to say sorry about yesterday. It was all kind of a mess. I still had the anxiety of getting through the first day and took it out on you." I look down at my feet, the classic Sadie move, and hold one of my hands to my other wrist and nervously rub it. "If you still wanted to have an ally, I'd love too."
"Really?" He asks nodding his head in a growing excitement, visible to anyone who looks at him.
"Sure." I look up at him and give a wry smile. "What's the plan?" I ask simply.
"Well, since today is the only 'double day' other than the season finale, there has to be some sort of 'double prize' or 'double time' sort of thing." Alessandro begins.
"Go on." I nod my head.
"Knowing FOTR, there has to be a down side to all this double stuff too. Maybe if we made a secret alliance, just the two of us, and only voted out other people's designs, we'd be safe and that would be two votes away from us." Alessandro explains cautiously.
"Okay. That'll work but how will we know whose designs are ours?" I ask thinking it through.
 "Embroidery."

Chapter 22

"Embroidery? I don't think we have the right-" I begin but Alessandro interrupts me by flicking a switch on his machine and the needle starts embroidering my initials on a sample piece of fabric Alessandro has under his machine.

"Whoa." I say in awe.

"Our machines have all the settings a regular machine would have, plus embroidery, hemming, and some more stuff. If we could make a small embroidery stitch in the corner of one of our designs of the other's initials, we would know whose is whose. You get it now?"

"I see. That way, we'll both be safe. But embroidery takes time though. It'll add a good five minutes of our time." I say back to him.

"Just make a design that isn't sloppy but isn't the best either. That way, you won't get voted out and you'll have time to embroider."

"Got it." I reach out my hand. "Allies?"

"Allies." He shakes my hand firmly.

We walk off to our sections and await Aliya's instructions. In the meantime, I grab sample pieces of fabric and practice the embroidery setting on the machine. When I've done about twenty of Alessandro' initials on the sample pieces, more contestants start coming to the stage for go time. I wave at Tiny on the way to the trashcan to throw out my sample pieces of Alessandro' initials. She waves back a little nervously and walks to her section. I do the same and walk over to mine and, again, await Aliya's call.

I look up from my section and see the huge window above the seating area that overlooks the main stage from Ying's department. I wonder how long it took her to sew all those amazing outfits and coats. I could never sew that much. I look back down to see all the contestants have gathered. Skylar gives me a dirty look and turns her head the other direction. Aliya walks up to her chair and sits down with a megaphone in her hand.

"Brandon. Make your way to center stage." Aliya barks. "Camera's rolling in three, two, one, action."

Brandon walks out from behind the curtains and waves to the imaginary people sitting all around him. He tightens his sequin blue jacket and takes a seat in his normal interview chair.

"Hey, hey, hey America. Welcome to Fashion on the Run: New York." He pauses as if he's awaiting applause from the imaginary audience. "Today is, the one and only, 'Double Diva Day.'" He pauses as more imaginary applause brings on a grin to his face. "As far as 'Double Diva Day' works, there's double the prizes, double the sewing, and the best part, double elimination."

At the last part I gasp. How could I not have thought about that before?

"Our remaining contestants that will be playing on 'Double Diva Day' are Lucy Davis, Ivy Smith, Stella Wilson, Clara Campbell, Trinity Brown, Sadie Benton, Alessandro Cipresso, Autumn Torres, Victoria Johnson, Emily Garcia, and Skylar Jones. On 'Double Diva Days,' they'll be three rounds of sewing assignments, each different for each Double Diva Day." Brandon explains.

"Instead of voting for the person you want out of the game, you'll be voting for who you want to stay in the game. Whoever gets the most votes per each round, gets a prize of their choice off of a list projected onto the screen. When they select their choice, they will be awarded with their prize. As for the first round of playing, the person with the least votes will not get voted off the show but will have to get a punishment, which will also be projected on the screen. Once they select their punishment, the game will move on. As for the last two rounds, the person with the least number of votes for each round will, sadly, go home after the round ends. Who's ready to play, Fashion on the Run: New York, Double Diva style?"

Brandon turns to the contestants and we all yell. "Yes."

"Well let the game begin." A projection pops up on the screen. "Your category is, Prom Outfits."

The dividers launch out of the ground and I immediately dive into my fabric bin, determined to do three things: make a good impression on the audience, win a prize this round, and not get a punishment. It seems fairly easy to me. I dig through my bin rapidly and make a big mess in my section. I keep digging until I find a neon pink sequin fabric, kind of like the blue one Brandon wears. I hold it in my hands and my brain takes over just as it always does. It makes the pattern in my head and my hands move with it. I step on all the fabrics I threw on the floor and get to my machine.

I sit in the chair and cut my fabric with the scissors in my drawer. When I finish cutting, I slip the cut pieces into my machine and seam them together. When I finish the seaming and hemming, I dig through the fabrics left in my bin and find a black tulle material and I stitch it onto the skirt of my dress to give it a bubble affect. I finish with exactly three minutes remaining and I turn to the machine again to sew in the initials. Instead of doing Alessandro' initials, I begin to second guess the plan and I start to sew a golden rose onto the side. I move quickly and embroider a beautiful golden rose onto the side of my bubble dress. If I'm going to win this, it has to be fair. I finish in exactly three minutes.

"Hands off your designs." Brandon announces. "Please put them on your mannequins and leave the rest to me." I do as I'm told and I place my short, pink and black, bubble dress onto the mannequin and await the staff members.

"Please step up to your podiums and take your vote." Brandon instructs us.

I walk up to my podium as it glows with the vibrant designs. I scroll through the designs and look very carefully for the golden initials Alessandro and I talked about. I find the golden initials on a handsome black coat with a vibrant red tie. *Ok. That one.* I think. But then, I scroll back through the prom outfits and decide to vote on one that catches my eye. A long green and blue metallic dress that goes down past my ankles. I imagined it shimmering as a girl wearing it dances gracefully across the dance floor that Gerta and I created. I can see the lights of the dance floor reflecting off of the metallic dress. This is the winner for this round. I hope so. Sorry Alessandro.

"All the votes, are now in." Brandon says a few minutes later. "Now, I'll ask a few contestants to come chat with me before the places are announced. Let's start with, Sadie Benton."
I start to walk out to center stage with Brandon when I see Aliya flailing her arms around crazily. She's warning me of something. Brandon gets the cue.
"Right after this." Brandon shouts quickly but in a calm manner.
The camera man cuts to commercial break and Aliya starts yelling. "Sadie. Why don't you have a mic? That's rule number one. Go to all the departments *before* you get onto stage. Rick. Rick. We have an emergency."
Rick comes running in with my bright green microphone in his hand. He runs straight up to me and tapes the mic to my face. "I thought I didn't see you today. Get back to your section. I cut out the part where you left and started walking. So, just go back to your section and act like you're just walking out. Got it? Now, get out there." Rick scurries off of the stage and I scurry back to my section.
"Action again in three, two, one." Aliya shouts.
I walk calmly to center stage and sit in the white interview chair. "Hello, Brandon." I say,
"Hello there, Sadie. Tell me, how confident are you feeling about your design today?"
"Well, so far, I'm feeling good. There's been nothing too hard yet." I shrug.

"Well, let's fix that. Yet is the magic word. I specifically pulled you out to talk because you've won something, or possibly lost something. As all the contestants' mannequins get pulled back out, we'll reveal your spot. Now, Clara, come join me out here." Brandon finishes and waves Clara over to the chair. I get out of my seat and walk back to my section. Next to me, Alessandro gives me a thumbs up and I take a deep breath in, and blow it out. I've either won, or lost something. I cross my fingers for the best until Brandon finishes with Clara.

"Now, Sadie and Clara, please stand below the screen for your placements." Brandon stands up and walks under the screen in the back of the room. Clara and I get up too and follow him to the screen.

"Are you guys ready?" Brandon shouts to the audience and Clara and I.

"Let's do this." I say quietly, but loud enough for my microphone to pick up.

"Sure." Clara says, also, quietly.

"Well, let's start with the winner of this round. Drumroll, please." Brandon says to the imaginary audience. "Sadie Benton."

I gasp in delight and do little jumps as my black hair bounces with me.

"I can tell you're excited. Now, shall we see the prizes?" Brandon asks, doing a perfect job as a TV game show host.

"Yes." I yell, a little too jumpy. But who cares? I won this first round and I'll show people that I'm proud of it. I'll get our old house back, no matter what. And this is just a step closer.

The screen glows and projects my list of options. When my eyes read the options, I realize this'll be a hard decision.

"Now, I see your reaction. It's a hard choice, yes. Shall I read your options?" Brandon pauses and starts reading out loud. "As everyone already knows, you can only pick one. So, will you choose, safety for a whole week straight, team up with a partner and get double points for the rest of the season and safety for your partner for the next week, get the newest sewing machine with all new features, a bonus hour on which you can start sewing early and get a big jump ahead, you get to choose the category for a whole episode, or, you get to choose one eviction today?" Brandon explains.

"Oh. That's a hard one." I say and think. If I get safety for a whole week starting now, I'll be safe all of today and next week's episode. But, if I team up with Alessandro, we can work together and get double points for the next and last final Double Diva Day. Although, if I choose the newest sewing machine, I'll be able to work faster and better and have a better embroidery setting. Ugh. Then, if I choose a bonus hour, I'll have plenty of time to perfect my design and have more time to add details, all without the new sewing machine. How will I ever decide. There's more too. If I choose the category for a whole episode, I can choose something I specialize in and I can beat all the other contestants. Lastly, if I choose to evict someone today, it'll be a feather in my cap because someone, like Skylar, who could really mess up my streak, will get voted out. I've already betrayed Alessandro once today by not picking his design. Then, if I don't pick the team join up, he'll think that I can't be trusted and eventually discover I didn't vote for him to stay today. Also, if he had won this round, he'd pick the team join up, so, should I? I could really use that eviction or safety for the next week. Should I do one of those or the team join up? I can't do this.

I turn and look at Alessandro and I can tell he'll be fine with whatever I choose. But then, he'll be safe and when people try to target him, he'll still be safe. All of the sudden, the words come out of my mouth without another second to think about all the decisions.

"I choose to team up with a partner." I say strongly.

I can see Alessandro beam at me from inside his dimmed glass divider. Those pearly white teeth are hard to miss. In the audience, I can hear the other contestants gasp at my decision.

"What?"

"Why would she do that?"

I hear from the other contestants. Only I will ever know why though. I want to show the audience that I'm a team player and won't choose to fight for only myself. This way, I'll make a huge impression and let people know who I really am, just like Aunt Kara told me.

Chapter 23

"Well done, Sadie. Now, who do you choose to work with?" Brandon asks me.

With that question, I pause. I know I've decided Alessandro but what about Tiny? We haven't seen each other today or after the show yesterday. Will she think I betrayed her? Will she think I don't want to be friends with her anymore? The last thing I want to do is mess up any friendships again. Those pickles are hard to get out of. Then, I do the only logical decision. "I'd like to work with Alessandro, please." I say, we have an alliance and I have to do what's best for my game.

"Beautiful." Brandon shouts into his handheld mic. "Now, for the punishment on Clara."

The screen changes to a list of bad punishments. Like bad, bad. "OH no." I hear Clara say.

"Oh yes." Brandon says back. "Shall I read these allowed? Will you choose to either, have an hour loss of time, get and old-fashioned sewing machine that doesn't have any newer settings, get your face revealed on your design so everyone knows what designs you made, or, be automatically eliminated but leave with a five-hundred-dollar reward?"

"I can't do this." Clara cries. "Fine. I'll do the reveal my face on all my designs." She sighs and walks back to her section, visibly failing and utterly defeated.

When I walk back to my section, everyone's giving me dirty looks I can't help but grin at. I'm victorious. When I actually get back to my section, the divider between Alessandro and I goes down and we combine our sections together to make one.

"You ready?" He whispers.

"Can't wait." I whisper excitedly back to him.

"For round two, our first elimination round, your category is," Brandon pauses and waits for the screen to change. "Casual picnic. Your time starts in three, two, one." A loud buzzer sounds as I get to work digging through my fabric bin.

"Look. Here." Alessandro pulls out his fabric bin, which is filled with different fabrics, and I find a cute light blue denim fabric and a cute yellow flower fabric as well.

"Can I use these?" I ask Alessandro.

"Go. We're running out of time." He yells back.

I bring the fabric back to my machine and start with the denim fabric first. I cut using my imaginary pattern and cut straight down the middle and make two identical pieces in the denim fabric. I go inside of the supply bin where I find my scissors and dig through to find some buttons. I find eight identical looking buttons, just a little different in size. *Perfect.* I think. I start sewing seams and ripping them to give the what's-becoming-shorts a nice ripped style. I sew a few real seams and then I finish the base and hem it so there's no strings hanging out in the places I don't want them to be. I hand stitch four buttons that get smaller in descending order down the middle of the shorts. Biggest button on the top, littlest button on the bottom. A perfect button-fly. Then, I start cutting again using the yellow flower fabric and cut to, again, identical pieces that will soon form a shirt. I seam them together to make a cute crop top with the remaining four little buttons closing up the V-neck. I embroider my little golden rose on the bottom right side of my shorts and pants.

After I finish, I hang them up on the mannequin and walk over to Alessandro' machine where he sits working hard on basically a boys' version of my outfit. Long denim pants with a gingham blue long-sleeve top. They'll match perfectly. Double points for us. Now that we are officially teamed up, he longer adds his tiny monogram. He puts his outfit on his mannequin and waits for the buzzer. We have exactly five minutes and nineteen seconds until the buzzer. Phew.

After the time's up, Alessandro and I wheel our mannequins up to the front of our section by our podiums. The staff members come and take our mannequins backstage and the podiums light up with the other outfits. Red gingham skirts, short pink gingham dresses, I think everyone got the gingham idea.

The buzzer rings and everyone jumps with a sudden startle. Everyone already knows the drill, so we all put our clothes on our mannequins and stand at our podiums. Mine glows a bright blue light that reflects off of my face. I scroll through everyone's designs. I notice that Alessandro' design has a big red X on it so people know they can't vote his out. Then, right next to the big red X, is a little denim and plaid jumpsuit that has Clara's picture in the bottom right-hand corner. I scroll back through the designs one last time and click on a very random, super sparkly, bright pink sequin dress with overalls. It doesn't fit the style one bit. After I submit my answer, it takes about another thirty seconds for the others to vote. When all the votes are in, the mannequins are brought back in, just like last time.

"Well done contestants. Our winner of the second prize of the day is," Brandon pauses and looks up at the screen. "Skylar Jones." Her smirky little face pops up on the screen and she struts up to the screen to pick her prize, making sure she bumps me on the way there.

"Well done, Skylar." Brandon claps loudly for all to hear.
"Thank you." She says and does a little baby face at the
camera.
"Would you like to see your prize options?" Brandon
asks inquisitively.
"Would I?" The screen glows with prize options just as
Skylar finishes her sentence. "Let's see."
"Your options are-" Brandon begins just to let Skylar
interrupt him.
"Why don't I get the same options as Sadie?" She yells.
"Well, every person gets a different list of things due to
the things you're into, your style, the live video feed,
etcetera." Brandon explains.
"Well, I'm here to play. My one option that I really want
from Sadie's board is to eliminate someone." She says
abruptly.
"Is that your one wish?" Brandon asks.
"Is it? Duh." Skylar says rudely.
"Well, we can give you one prize option from Sadie's
board. How's that?"
"Will I get to pick it?"
"Well of course not, Skylar. It'll be selected randomly.
Want to get something off of Sadie's board?" Brandon
asks excitedly. I can feel the people watching through
their TV's stuffing popcorn in their mouth right this
second.
"I'll take it." Skylar says. "Anything from Sadie." She
adds in a whisper. Why does she dislike me so much?
"Alrighty tidy. We'll show you your option, right after
this." Brandon says as the camera cuts to a commercial.
"B.R.B." Brandon runs backstage and comes running
back in a very long two minutes.
"We're back on in three, two, one." Aliya shouts.
"Welcome back, America. Where were we?" Brandon
says jokingly to pull the strings of suspense.

"You were giving me *my* prize." Skylar grumbles as she crosses her arms.

"Oh yes. Of course, we were. Here's how it'll work; you'll pull one card from my hand," Brandon pulls a bunch of cards out of his sleeve. He's like a magician on camera. "Then, it'll reveal one prize from Sadie's board that you can choose."

"I believe it's double diva day." Alessandro chimes in.

"On it my boy." Brandon yells happily. "There's one unlucky card in the pile that has an automatic elimination. All the rest are an extraordinary prize, off of the one and only, Sadie Benton's board. Still want to play?"

"No. You never mentioned-" Skylar starts.

"Just kidding. You have no choice, Miss Skylar. You choose when you choose and now there's no way out of it. Pick a card, any card." Brandon fans out the cards in his hand all face down so no one can see them except for the microscopic looking camera on his shoe. Only us contestants can see it.

Skylar reaches out and pulls a card second to last on the left side of the fan. *Please be elimination. Please be elimination.* Then, she screams.

Chapter 24

Skylar screams and screams and screams. It sounds like someone's been murdered in the studio with how loud it is. Or is it a scream of happiness? Skylar starts screaming even louder and stomping her feet against the ground then jumping up high. No one can tell what's happening. Her blonde waves bounce as she jumps, her blue eyes locked with the words written on the card. I can feel all the eyes of America staring right here, and it makes me anxious. Skylar keeps screaming. Louder and more high pitch with every second. Her scream echoes throughout the studio and it rings in my ears. She suddenly stops screaming, drops the card, and faints. My automatic instinct is to rush over and check that she's breathing. I run right over but instead stop and stare at her card. *New sewing machine.* Instead, I don't care. I continue on my path to Skylar to make sure she's alright. I put two fingers out and search for the pulse in her neck. I press it right to the spot my first-aid class teacher told me. *Boom.* Three seconds. *Boom.* Five seconds. Then, I start screaming. This isn't normal.

"Help. Help. She's dying." It's the only words I could make come out of my mouth. "Help. Someone. Anyone." Brandon and the other contestants rush out to help. I keep my fingers on her neck and feel her pulse beating slower and slower by the second. "Alessandro. Get someone. Help. Please." He rushes backstage and for after a very long thirty seconds returns with the medical-aides.

"Help. Fast." He yells as he jogs back center stage, the medics close behind.

They immediately drop at her side and feel her pulse.
Then, one starts doing CPR. I start sweating. Is she *dead*?
The thought echoes in my head over and over. *Please no.
Oh, please no.* I turn and see the camera still rolling. I run
back to my section and grab a piece of fabric and cover
her face. She wasn't my best friend but she wasn't
someone I wanted dead. The moment lasts forever before
more medics show up and put her onto a stretcher and
carry her out of the building.
"The show must go on." Brandon shouts to the camera.
"Are you kidding." I burst. "Skylar might have just
died."
I see Aliya waving her hands like crazy signaling for me
to stop, for the camera to stop rolling, for Brandon to stop
talking and for the feed to be cut.
"No. If the show goes on, I'm out of here." The words
come out before I had time to see what I'd just
announced to America. "If Skylar's dead because of this,
I'm gone. Zero, zilch, nada. Done." I shout.
The stage door opens and Skylar's family runs in.
"Skylar. My baby." Her mom shouts. Her dad follows
closely behind, speechless.
Her mom's words strike me. If I were to have kids
someday, this would be the worst possible thing ever. Her
words bring me tears. Tears of power.
"No. The show stops now. This isn't going on until
Skylar returns." I yell the camera. The camera slowly
fades out and ends the episode with one last shot of
everyone's faces, startled and scared, kneeling on the
floor where Skylar was two minutes ago.
Skylar's mom runs up to me. "Sadie. Are you Sadie
Benton?" Her mom cries.
"Um, yes, mam." I say, as calmly as I can, despite all
that's happened.
"Where is she?" She asks desperately.

"I think she was taken to the hospital. I'm so sorry." I say
with a tear in my eye.
Then, out of nowhere, a spider comes crawling off of the
card Skylar was holding. Her mom screeches.
"A recluse spider." Her mom whispers. "Her doctor
warned me of this. She's highly allergic to the venom. I
thought it was never a possibility because they're so
rare." Then, her mom bursts into tears. As does Tiny, and
Victoria, and Clara, and Emily, and everyone else in the
whole entire room.
"We have to get to the hospital. Stat." I order. I jump
outside the door of the stage and flag a taxi over.
"Where's the nearest hospital?" I ask the driver urgently.
"Just down the street, and take a left, then turn-"
"Perfect. Take us there. Now." Everyone jumps inside the
car and the driver drives slowly down the road, stopping
at every single stop light. I start banging my fist on his
chair. "Move it." With this he takes off into the distance.
When we get there, we all pile out of the car and we run
to the front desk.
"Skylar. We're here for Skylar Jones." I pant.
The lady at the front desk moves without a sound or
expression and leads us up a staircase to the third level
and knocks on a room door. She opens the door and lets
us all file in. Skylar lays there, motionless. I go up to try
to feel her pulse but a sudden voice stops me.
"Don't touch her." I whip my head around and turn to
face a doctor whose eyes are very concerned.
"I…I was just going to feel her pulse." I start to explain.
"Look." He points up to a little screen with a radar on it
that makes a little beeping sound every once in a while.
"That's her?" Tiny asks. "Her heart beat? It doesn't look
right."
"Indeed." The doctor replies as he studies something on a
computer.

"Is she okay?" Her mom wails.

"For right now." The doctor says calmly.

"Right now? She's going to die?" Her mom wails again.

"It appears that she's suffering from Anaphylaxis. Does anyone know what she came in contact with?" The doctor asks.

"Yes. She was bitten by a highly poisonous spider." Her mom screams. "She's allergic to *the spider.*"

"I see." He types something calmy onto the computer.

"I think we need to do something quickly." Tiny announces impatiently. She walks up to Skylar's bed and frantically presses the button to call the nurse.

"Wait. What are you doing?" The doctor starts.

"I'm doing what needs to be done." Tiny sees an EpiPen and quickly jams it into Skylar's thigh.

"How did you-," stammers the doctor.

Several nurses rush into the room to help as the useless doctor exits. Skylar's parents hug Tiny, tears filling up their eyes.

Slowly the beeping on the screen gets louder and more frequent. Tiny looks hopeful.

"Now, we wait." Tiny tells us.

Chapter 25

After ten long minutes of the beeping happening more and more frequently, Skylar's eyes blink open to a bloodshot blue. Skylar's parents rush up to her bedside and squeeze her hands and give her big hugs.

"Careful not to overwhelm her." Tiny warns.

I rush up to her and stand over her, speechless. Then, she knocks her mom and dad aside and hurls her weak body towards me. I jump backwards in surprise. "Tiny, what's going on?" I ask.

"I would slowly step back out of the room. Everyone except her parents. Her body is still weak from the venom and she may not respond well for some more time." Tiny backs off slowly as she explains. I get in line and we all walk outside of Skylar's room except for her parents.

"You were amazing in there Tiny." Clara gasps in awe.

"How do you know this much about medical things?" Alessandro asks, bewildered by her skills.

"Well, I told everyone that my family lives on a farm, right? Well, anyway, it's not just a normal farm. My parents are both farm veterinarians and take in hurt of wounded farm animals. Since I'm the oldest in my family still living at the farm, my parents have been taking me under their wing as a medical student. It turns out, humans have a lot of similarities to farm animals, such as severe allergic reactions to foods and venomous bites, particularly the little rats that hide in the small holes in the barn." Tiny gives a little shrug.

"What about that whole thing with the needle?" Ivy asks.

"Oh. The Epinephrine?" It's the only quick and effective way to treat someone having a life-threatening allergic reaction." Tiny answers, sounding much older and wiser than her age.

Everyone nods in agreement although we have no clue what she is talking about.

"I think I have to start getting back to the hotel, my parents will be worried." Emily announces. "Will Skylar be fine here alone?"

"She won't be alone. She needs time to rest and recover. I'll stay the night here. Could you let my mom know, Emily?" Tiny says.

"Sure. I promise to stop by again tomorrow. Bye." Emily jogs down the hall and down the stairs.

"I think I better get going as well."

"Me too."

"Me three." The group starts saying. After a few minutes, it's only Tiny, Alessandro, Lucy, and I left at the hospital with Skylar.

"I didn't think anything like this could ever happen on a sewing show." Lucy says halfheartedly.

"Yeah." I agree. "It was kind of a lot. I was actually starting to freak out there for a minute." I added.

"Me as well." Says Alessandro.

"I know this is a little off topic," Lucy starts. "But I want to get my mind off of this whole thing. Anyway, how did you start sewing, Alessandro?"

"Me? Well, my family grew up in Venice, Italy and we owned a mask shop that was fairly popular. My dad trained my brother and I to run the shop. He taught us everything like sewing, customer management, custom orders, etcetera. When my older brother turned eighteen, he took the shop into his own hands so my mom, dad, and I moved to America."

"You do a good job of hiding your accent." Tiny jokes with her huge country accent.

"Well, I never really had one to begin with." Alessandro shrugs.

"That explains a lot." Lucy laughs.

"You've been awfully quiet, Sadie." Tiny adds, placing her arm on my shoulder.

"It's just a lot to take in. I've never been this close to a medical emergency before. I always see it on the news or hear Mark and Peter talk about their medical training in school."

"I agree. It *is* a lot to deal with at first but you start getting used to it. Besides running a farm for injured animals, a lot of stuff goes down with having twelve younger siblings. By the way, what are your brothers studying in school?"

"Well, their training for the military, actually. They have to pass a ton of classes like medical classes, agility classes and some other stuff I don't really know about. I think they learn medical in case someone gets hurt." I try to explain the best I can.

"Wow. That's a big job to take on." Lucy tells me.

"Yeah. I don't want them to go away. It's kind of scary to think about." I tell them, careful not to sound too weak on my own.

We all look up to see Skylar's parents walking out of her room towards us, sobbing.

"Thank you, guys. You are all life savers." Skylar's mom tells Alessandro, Lucy, Tiny and I. "Especially you." Skylar's mom nods at me. "And Tiny, your medical skills are quite amazing."

"Thank you." I look down at my feet as Skylar's parents walk away into a waiting room. Then, I look at the clock above Skylar's room and see it's getting late. I should probably be getting back home. I open the small curtain that leads into Skylar's room and stick my head in. She's resting quietly and still looks weak and pale. I whisper goodnight and close the door.

As I exit Skyler's room, Alessandro and Lucy give me a hug goodbye and Tiny waves at me as she heads into the waiting room with Skyler's parents.

I walk down the stairs to the lobby and the rude lady at the front desk. "May I use your phone? I need to phone my parents."

"You came here alone?" The lady asks suspiciously.

"Well, with some friends."

"This is no place for teenagers to be messing around." The lady says loudly. *Great. My luck with front desk people these last few days.*

"No. It's not like that." I start to explain. "I came here with my friends because one of the girls got bit by a spider and,"

"No more. What a stupid excuse, young lady. You need to leave. Teenagers are not allowed alone in the hospital without an adult." She points to the door. "Out. Get out now."

I rush out the door and look at the crowded sidewalks full of people. I notice a clothing shop just across the street and decide to settle down there for a bit. I can grab some clothes and go to a fitting room just to lock myself in somewhere safe. I stand at the stop light and wait for the green walk signal. When it finally turns green, the cars keep blasting through the intersection. It turns red again and I'm stuck waiting for the green walk light. At the next green walk signal, again, nobody stops. I watch as the other New Yorkers calmy cross through the intersection and the cars finally stop. I wait for the next light cycle and begin to carefully cross with the crowd of people so I can blend in. Then, a car comes to a sudden halt beside me. The person rolls down their windows. All four.

"Are you Sadie Benton?" The lady driving the car asks.

"Um. Yes?" I say sounding like it's a question. I'm getting a bad feeling. I'm sure Lucy or Alessandro wouldn't have minded me coming to their hotel room and taking shelter for a bit longer while I get a hold of Aunt Kara or Mom.

"We know the way to your house. Want a ride?"

Rule number one for everyone: stranger danger. "No thanks. I'm fine from here." I answer politely.

"You sure? I work with your aunt at her studio. You can trust me. I have a seat in the back open."

"Um. I'm fine. Really. Thanks." *Stop talking, brain.*

"Come on. I don't bite." The lady pushes.

Where's the busy crowd? I have to take a risk. I would rather get hurt by a car than being abducted as a fourteen-year-old. I take off down the street not caring about any of the cars speeding my way. All of them come to a sudden halt and I realize I created a traffic jam. I run into the clothes shop and close the door behind me. I run up to the girl at the counter.

"Hello, miss. How may I help you today?" She asks kindly.

"May I use your phone? I need to call my mom. Someone's trying to kidnap me outside." I say, out of breath.

"Oh dear. Here you go." She opens the little side door that leads behind the counter and I walk up to the phone. I type in my mom's number and it takes her a few seconds to pick up.

"Hello?" My mom asks.

"Mom."

"Sadie? Where are you? We've been so worried."

"I'm at a place, um. Hold on," I put the phone on my shoulder and look around the shop. "I'm at Fleur's Delicacies. I need help. Someone tried to take me outside, I think."

"I'm on my way. Remember, don't talk to strangers." She hangs up and I put the phone down.

"Thank you." I tell the girl. She doesn't look much older than me. Maybe sixteen?

"Of course. Your mom's on the way?"

"Yes."

"Alright. Do you want to wait outside?" She asks.

"Um, could I stand inside? Right here? Behind the desk? I'm scared of that person outside." I point to the busy street outside.

"Of course. You can sit right here." The girl pulls up a chair from under the counter and I gladly take a seat.

"Wait. Are you Sadie? Sadie Benton? From the F.O.T.R show?"

"Um. Yes. I am." I say a little uncomfortably. I like being famous but not in a way where people know me and want to abduct me.

"Oh. My. Gosh." The girl smiles, her smile so big, her lips are practically touching the bottom of her eyes. "I love your designs. I knew you would win from the start."

"Really? I might not win." I say modestly.

"Seriously. I LOVE your designs. After you get off the show, winner or not, are you starting a clothing line? I love your aunt too." She grabs the corner of her skirt and shows me the label: KaraCouture.

"Cool." I say,

"I can't believe I'm actually talking to you. I want to show you something." The girl walks out from behind the counter and grabs a shirt from a rack. She brings it back over to me behind the counter. "Take it. As a gift from me. And the Fleur's Delicacies team. We're huge fans of you."

I take the shirt out of her hand and see the graphic on the front. It has all of my designs printed out in vivid color starting with my silk dress. By the way the shirt is made, it looks like the dresses are drawn on a sheet of paper. All in the background behind the dresses are words: *Team Sadie. Number one. Go Sadie.*

It looks like it's written in pencil on the shirt to match the paper affect. "Thank you." I say as I admire the shirt.

"Can I get a photo with you? I want to show *all* my friends." She asks excitedly.

"Sure." I say happily. I feel more comfortable in the store but something still doesn't feel right. I love that there are actually some people that like me here. This is what I wanted, right? For people to think that I could actually win and think I'm strong enough to make it. This is exactly it. People are selling the *Team Sadie* shirts, people are buying them, people are cheering for me. Everything I wanted last night. What's wrong? I smile for the picture with the girl and I see my aunt's pearly black limo pull up outside.

"Thank you so much. I'll always remember this day. *Always.*" The girl tells me as she stares in awe at the picture on her phone.

"No. Thank you for letting me stay here. I think I have to get going though. I hope I'll see you around." I tell her.

"For sure. Thank you." The girl squeals. She opens the door to behind the counter to let me out and I walk outside, holding my Team Sadie shirt in my arms. Ronald gets out of the car and opens the door for me. I step inside the limo and see my whole family in there. Mark, Peter, Mom, and Aunt Kara.

"Hi." I say as I sit down.

My mom grabs me and wraps me in a huge hug. "What happened?"

I begin to try and explain to my family all that has happened. In that moment, I suddenly realize that, in the time where I felt like no one was on my side, everyone was.

Later that night, after I got home and had family dinner, I go to take a shower. I walk into the bathroom and strip down my fancy clothes from the shoot while I wait for the water to warm up. When I get in the shower, the water is scorching hot and makes my skin turn red because of the heat. But I don't care. I stand there in the shower, with burning hot water streaming over my bare body and don't care. Skylar, who was my enemy just four hours ago, is all I can think about now. I think about her poor parents, kneeled beside her hospital bed with the only skilled doctor being thirteen-year-old Tiny. When the thought comes back and every moment of the day replays in my head, I can't help it but to burst into tears. My brain automatically goes to how bad I've treated Skylar recently and how my family would react if *I* was in that situation. I cry and cry until my face is soggy from tears. I decide just to rub off the makeup and get out of the shower. I grab my towel and walk out into my room, and see the beautiful city beneath me. It's too beautiful for a time like this. A time of struggle and stress for so many people. Me, who bursts into tears in the shower. Tiny, who has to pull off an all-nighter at the hospital watching over Skylar. Skylar, who is in the hospital fighting for her life. The sun sets, bringing a shimmery glow over the Empire State Building. I look up, at the very tip of the building and see a cloud that has a silver lining. A real one. The gold glow forms a halo around the cloud that brings it to life, seeming to say to me, *"Tomorrow is a new day. Let it come."* Then the cloud moves on and the sun goes on below the horizon. Tomorrow *is* a new day.

Chapter 26

In the morning, I wake to find myself laying on the floor
next to the window-wall with my wet bath towel still
covering me. I stand up and stretch, welcoming the new
day. I drop off my towel in the bathroom and head down
to my closet to get dressed. Today, I decide on one of my
old shirts, full of memories. My black and white AC/DC
shirt. I stare at it before I put it on and think of the time I
went over to Addy's house and all the music on her CD
album was AC/DC. I remember then how we went
shopping with Marie and we all picked out matching
AC/DC shirts when we were at least ten. I've only grown
a few inches since then so the shirt still fits and it's been
a tradition that each one of us wears our matching shirt
on the first, second, or third day of school, the first day of
Summer, the last day of winter break, and on New Year's
Eve. I throw it on and grab a plain pair of shorts and
Vans. When I get back up to my room, I run a quick
brush through my hair and head out the door of my room.
I find Mark, sprawled out on the floor of the video game
room, crushing Peter on a game of 30-1. When they see
me standing at the doorway, they both wave at me, letting
me know everything's going to be alright. I enter the
living room and find Mom sitting at a chair reading some
of the mail Aunt Kara got.
"Morning, Mom." I say, a little melancholy.
"Morning, hon. How're you doing?"
"I mean…" I trail off and start crying again as I rush into
her arms for comfort.
"It'll all be alright. Ok? This is a lot to handle." She tries
to tell me knowingly.

"I know." I cry. After a few minutes of me hugging my mom tightly, I let her know I'm going out today and head down the elevator to the parking garage. In the parking garage, Ronald is already waiting for me, so I just hop in the car.

"Where can I take you? Your mother called down to let me know to meet you here."

"Could I get to the hospital, please?" I say.

"You sure you don't want to go somewhere more fun?" He asks considerately.

"I'm sure. Although I need you to walk me in so I don't get kicked out for being there without an adult."

He nods turns the mirror above the navigation map so he can see me. I can feel his stare, even through his dark shades that he wears. "You got it Sadie."

I gaze out the window. Shops are bustling and busy with customers scattering everywhere. People are running around with their arms overflowing with bags and shoe boxes. People are crossing the street while cars rush by.

"You like it here, princess?" Ronald asks me, interrupting my thoughts.

I sit there for a minute, pondering my life since I've moved here. "Aunt Kara has a great house." I say,

"She sure does. The one and only." He replies in a mood that makes me have to smile. "There's that smile. Well, I guess that concludes our ride because we've arrived. I'll walk you in and will wait in the lobby. Just take your time. I'm in no rush." He tilts his glasses down and winks at me through the mirror.

"Thank you." I say as I get out of the car. I see the dull
parking lot just outside the hospital entrance and across
the street, the shop I ran into for safety. I look back at
Ronald trailing behind me as I make my way through
probably the least busiest parking lot in New York to the
entrance of the hospital. When I enter, I recognize the
receptionist the minute I see her.
"Here for Skylar Jones." She says rudely. It sounds like
she really hates her job.
"Yes."
"I see that you brought a chaperone this time. Follow me
this way." She leads me up an elevator to the seventh
floor and lets me off. "Room 207 on the left."
I don't bother to say anything as I make my way to the
room. Just a few doors down, I find room 207 and knock
on the door. Skylar's dad answers.
"Hi Sadie." I notice the sleep lines under his eyes. The
moment I get inside the room, I see Tiny and Skylar's
mom, next to her bed. I sit on the stool on the opposite
side of the bed. Skylar is asleep. Sounds like she slept
through the night, that must be a good sign? I sit there for
a few minutes, feeling useless in this room when Skylar
wakes up.
"Sadie." Skylar says at she slowly and weakly sits up
with a smile. I smile back and hold her hand.
"She still has a long way to go." Chimes Tiny. She has
developed an infection from the spider bite and will have
to stay here to heal and recover. She's not out of the
woods just yet.
The next few weeks go by like this and my stops to the
hospital become more regular. An occasional call once or
twice a day back home also becomes part of my daily
schedule.

After a good four weeks, with a new episode of Fashion on the Run: New York every week, only six contestants remain. So far, the people who've gone home are Ivy, Emily, Chloe, Stella, Autumn, and of course Skylar. We've formed little groups amongst ourselves for the competition, Tiny and Lucy, Victoria and Clara, and lastly Alessandro and I. Victoria and Clara are by far the best group out of us. Probably the most fashionable too. If it were up to America, they would win the whole game. The first round of the night is to sew an outfit to wear for a long period of time in the wild. Alessandro has been doing most of the sewing while I pin together and exercise the fabrics to find the ones that look best together. After Alessandro sews the last bit of fabric together, we dress up our mannequin in a dark orange shirt with a rainproof jacket and some jeggings that have secret pockets just about everywhere you can imagine with exactly twenty-nine seconds left. We wheel our mannequin up by our voting screen and put the screen up over it so the other contestants can't see our design. When everyone is done, it's time to vote. Alessandro and I both go to our screens and view the options. Long-sleeve farmer overalls with a plain black shirt under it or a dress that has sequins all over it but with a single button on the center that makes it turn into a dark green jumpsuit. I know exactly what team did what. I look at Alessandro and we both decide on the sequin dress/green jumpsuit.

"The votes are now all in." Brandon announces. He receives an envelope from one of the backstage staff members and opens it dramatically. "The team, who will be leaving us tonight is, Victoria and Clara. Victoria and Clara, could you please join me at the meeting chairs? The other contestants, you know what to do."

As I head backstage with Tiny, Lucy, and Alessandro, we all gather in the party room, though none of us are feeling it, to grab a snack and watch the interview.

"Now, how are you two feeling?" Brandon asks sympathetically.

"I…I just really thought we would make it to the end." Victoria says, confidently despite the surprising eviction.

"I did too. I felt we were *the* team America was looking for to represent youth fashion designers." Clara says sadly.

"Yes. I believe we all did. Now Clara, how did the rest of the show go considering your flump at Double Diva night?" Brandon asks considerably.

"Well, it was a little painful because that brought down Victoria too since we joined forces at week eight." Clara answers.

"Ah. Yes. Victoria, did you ever second guess yourself after teaming up with Clara because of this punishment?"

"Actually, I did. A few times I was thinking that maybe that would put a sheer target on our backs but surprisingly, no one saw that target until four weeks later."

"Yes. I understand your point very much." Brandon turns around to face the camera as he, very enthusiastically, wraps up the episode. "Well, America, that concludes the surprising elimination night on Fashion on the Run: New York." The theme song music then ends with Brandon smiling all cheesy at the camera followed by the ending credits.

"You guys all know what this means now, right?" Lucy asks sadly as she stares down at her shoes.

Then, we all stare down at our shoes. We'll all have to break up our teams and have another double elimination to conclude the whole season.

"Only one of us can win." Tiny adds, still looking at her shoes. At this, Tiny comes in and gives Lucy a big hug and I join in too. I look up at Alessandro and invite him in too.

"Is this too corny for you?" I ask.

He comes in and gives us all a hug. "Group hug." I say in my best five-year-old voice. At that, we all start laughing. It feels good to laugh again. Come to think of it, I don't think I've laughed since I met Thew back at home. Even though I miss home dearly, I'm starting to get used to this place and accepting the idea that I'm not going to make it through the end. All that matters now is nothing. We took the four of us to the finale so now whoever wins will be a win for all of us.

Chapter 27

The next few days go by in a blur but Thursday is the day everything goes down. I get to the hospital early that morning and head up to room 207 on the seventh floor like usual. When I open the door, doctors and surgeons are flustered all around Skylar and Skylar's mom is sitting in the corner crying with her face in her hands. To make the room even louder between all the talking and crying is the fact that the monitor that is beeping like crazy and different than it usually does.

"What's happening?" I try to yell over the noise. It's no use. I start walking deeper into the room when I feel a hand on my shoulder. Tiny.

"They've got her. We shouldn't be here." Tiny says calmly.

"What's happening?" I insist as Tiny drags me out of the room. She stops me right outside the room and puts her hands on my shoulders. "What, Tiny?"

"They were injecting a shot into her thigh and she flinched, the first time she's moved in days, and she had almost a full heart attack.

"Is it still happening?" I yell as I push through the doors to room 207.

"Sadie. No. You can't be in there. She's going to be seriously damaged after this. They were expecting a full recovery until this. There's no room for you in there." Tiny grabs me and tugs me back outside.

"It's all my fault." I cry.

"How's it your fault, sugar cube?" Tiny comforts me.

"Don't try to comfort me. I was the one that made her jealous so she could pick one of *my* amazing cards. I might've thought she deserved it at the time but now? Is she even going to recover at *all*?" I scream as I cry into my hands.

"Sadie. You're ok. None of that was your fault. She was being a brat then and there but now you see her differently and that's all that matters." Tiny tells me.
"What if I never get to…" I trail off as Tiny drags me into the elevator away from room 207. She sits with me outside on the bench and waits for me to calm down.
"When will we find out what's happening?"
"They should be done with her later tonight. I promise I'll stay overnight and keep an eye out." Tiny tells me.
"But tomorrow is one of the last episodes of F.O.T.R." I say,
"I know. I'll make it there in time." Tiny promises.
"Promise?"
"Promise." Tiny shakes my pinky. "You should head back home. Your brain isn't built for this kind of stuff."
"Oh, shut up." I say as I stand up and wipe the last remaining tears out of my eyes. When I get into the car, I don't say another word and neither does Ronald. He just silently drives me back to the apartment and drops me off. He must know that this isn't the right time to talk. I press the elevator button up to the top floor and walk straight into the room I know I'll be the happiest. Mark and Peter's video game room. The only thing I say when I get inside is "Controller." And open my hand for them to pass it to me. All day, I take turns crushing Mark and him crushing me but no matter what, Peter is always at the very bottom, winning off of no one, defeated by everyone.
The next morning I hear, "Rise and…" Mark starts.
"How are you already up?"
"Magic." I reply sarcastically.
"Whoa there, grumpy. One of the staff at FOTR, Ying, I think it was, told Aunt Kara to send you in your PJ's because she has something special planned today."

"Sounds good." I give Mark a thumbs up as I push the door closed. I head into the bathroom and brush my teeth, throw on some comfy slides that I forgot to put up from yesterday and head out the door with Aunt Kara.

"Good luck out there." Mark tells me on the way out.

"Break a leg." Peter yells at me. "Or maybe a finger would be better. That way I can beat your fast fingers at the controller." Peter adds.

"Love you, hon. You'll do great." Mom hugs and kisses me. "We'll be right here waiting for you on your way back."

The elevator door closes and wooshes Aunt Kara and I down to the parking garage where Ronald awaits us.

"Morning, Miss Kara. Morning, princess." Ronald says.

"Morning, Ronald. The FOTR studio if you wouldn't mind." Aunt Kara instructs.

"No problem, ma'am." As the car moves out of the parking garage, he strikes up a conversation. "Season finale?"

"No. Not yet. Next week though." I reply. "I doubt I'll make it that far."

"Ohh. Silly Sadie. You're the best one." Aunt Kara hugs me.

"Still, I honestly think that their next target is me after they break up the teams." I say,

"That's probably because you're too good for them." Ronald tells me as he peeks through the mirror.

"Exactly." Aunt Kara adds.

"We've arrived. Good luck out there, princess." Ronald gets out of the car and opens the door for me.

"Thank you."

"You got this, pumpkin." Aunt Kara yells as the door closes and Ronald gets back into the driver's seat.

As they pull away, I make my way to the entrance where Ying greets me.

"I see you follow orders." She stays sternly. I notice her eyes reflect a brief glimmer of sunlight. My curiosity gets the better of me.

"You haven't been outside for a while?" I ask curiously. Ying looks me flat in the eye. She stares at me in a very intimidating way. I keep staring back at her. Eventually, she moves on and walks at lighting speed up to her room at FOTR. I have to walk extra fast to catch up to her. When I get inside, I can't see her anywhere but then I hear the door slam closed behind me and the lock being imputed. I whip around and see her eyes glaring at me, still locking the door.

"What's happening?" I ask, starting to panic. I blink and she's gone. I hear a voice behind me and whip back around to find her, her face so close to mine, I can smell her breath through her nose.

"I was the one who put that spider on Skylar." She says deviously. The dark black dress she wears has extra-long sleeves that form a cup around her wrists. She turns over her hand to reveal the spider, like a little pet as it sits on her palm.

"What? Why would you do that?" I really start to panic. "I was trying to help you win. Her dress is where I put it. And this is how you repay me?" She starts to yell as her voice echoes through the dull room where it seems no echo could ever exist. I blink once more and she's gone. I turn around and find her back by the door. "I was trying to help you win this. When I was your age, FOTR tested me as one of their earliest competitors. I was defeated by a girl like Skylar and ended up here. I *helped* you by putting that spider in her dress. And *this* is how you repay me?"

"I...I don't understand." I stammer. *Don't blink. Don't blink.* I tell myself over and over.

"You know *exactly* what I'm talking about. You visit her every day. Like she's your *friend*."

"You could have killed her. You still can. Why would you do something like that? As much as I want to win, this was not how I wanted it to happen. I would never harm another human being to win a stupid prize." I yell. Ying seems a little stricken by this but keeps her cool. Too late. I blink. She moves this time and I feel a small tickle on my neck. I turn around and see that the spider has moved off of Ying's hand and is nowhere in sight. It's on my neck.

"Goodbye little one. Your time ends now." Ying says darkly as a blur comes into my vision. I try to snap out of it but it's no use.

"Ying. Ying." I vaguely hear Aliya's voice and energetic knocking on the door. "Do you have Sadie? We're on in thirty minutes and she needs to get her mic." The door handle jiggles. "Why is the door locked? Ying? Are you in there?"

As the blur continues, I can just form a single, faded, cry.

"Help."

Then, the blur consumes me as a whole.

Chapter 28

They're cars everywhere. Tipped over and on their side. There's a barrier that lays between me and a regular world. I watch as my teammates cross the border but become consumed and put into a spell where they defend the barrier, completely mind wiped. Thew walks up to the barrier and takes a short glance back at me. We lock eyes. I realize what he's doing. It's just me and one other person left on this side. He's sacrificing himself for me. "No." I yell. He looks away from me and faces the barrier as he walks through. I watch as his eyes turn into black pits as his whole life is washed away from him. "Thew." I say weakly. I reach my hand out and an image of Thew appears before me. His hand outstretched, touching mine though I feel nothing. I walk up to him. I place my hand gently on his cheek and search for the warmth I once felt inside of him. There's coldness instead.

"I know this is fake, Thew." I say, holding back tears. "But I've always wanted to do this." I stand on point and give him a long kiss right on the lips, my hands cradling his face. As I slowly back away, the version of Thew slowly dissolves to ashes starting from his legs, leaving his head the last thing to fade to ashes. My hand sits in the emptiness, now holding nothing…

"Sadie. Are you okay?" Tiny embraces me. "She's awake everyone. Hurry."

As I slowly open my eyes, I see a crowd of people, Aliya, Tiny, Lucy, Alessandro, Brandon. "I am ok." I give them a thumbs up. Everyone takes a huge sigh of relief and starts laughing.

"Great timing, Sadie. You were only asleep for twenty-five minutes." Aliya exclaims, checking her watch.

At that, I pop up. "We're on in five minutes."

"Oh no, Sadie. We've delayed the show a bit. All of you guys can just wear PJs for the episode today." Aliya explains.

"Good." I say, "What happened to Ying?"

Lucy points towards the front door and I see the police handcuffing Ying as she tries to escape. I stand up slowly, as does everyone else. I follow Ying outside the building, keeping a good distance away from her. As they try to shove Ying into the back of the police car, she resists.

"You." She yells at me as she resists more. "The reason I'm stuck up there was because of Kara." The police try to push her in the car more. "Kara. Curse you, Kara. Curse you." The police finally shove her into the car with enough force, she has no choice but to fall in the car.

I stand there as I watch the police car drive away with Ying in the back, still cursing at Aunt Kara. I walk back into the building, everyone fussing over me.

"What was that about?" Tiny asks.

"What did she do to you?" Lucy asks patting my back.

"Do you need me to delay the show further?" Aliya has her clipboard at the ready.

"Everyone, I think I'm fine. After all, the show must go on, right Brandon?" I stop the crowd.

After that, the crowd demolishes and leaves me with just Carrie and Rick. They nod at each other and get to work on me. By the time their done with me, it's exactly five minutes after the original time Aliya wanted to start.

Carrie says something into her walkie talkie and waves me out onto the stage. When I peek through the curtain, I see Brandon has already started the show and is giving everyone a review on what's happened over the last few weeks. When he finishes up, he opens his arms out wide and Tiny, Lucy, Alessandro and I all run out on the stage from different parts of the curtain, knowing it's our cue.

"Welcome. Welcome. With only four of you left, I know
exactly what you've been thinking. 'Oh no. Brandon's
going to break up the teams.' Am I right?"
All four of us nod and look at each other, knowing that is
never how anything goes in Brandon's book.
"Well, we won't be breaking up the teams." Brandon
exclaims, looking quite happy at our surprised faces.
"How will the voting work? It's going to be even?" Lucy
asks.
"Well, that's just the fun part. We're going to leave this
voting up to America." Brandon yells excitedly. He turns
around to face the camera. "Now, as for all of you folks,
you know you've heard it right. Log onto our YouTube
channel and there will be a live voting poll that opens up
at the second the timer goes off here in New York." He
gestures to the screen with a big timer counting down.
"So, for all you folks out there, you know what to do." At
that, both of the side doors open up by security guards
and clusters of two-hundred people at each door fill up
the red-velvet seats that have been empty this whole
season. Doors I never even knew existed on the second
floor also overflow with people, wearing fancier and
more exquisite clothing than the people at the seats down
stairs by the stage. I find my family at the upstairs seating
area wearing their finest clothing Aunt Kara probably
made or loaned them. Although, every time I look at
Aunt Kara, I don't see my aunt. I see the mean fourteen-
year-old that made Ying so devastated and defeated, she
felt the need for violence and to harm others. Brandon
has to talk extra loud for me to finally realize where I am
and how many people are watching me today.
"Now, the four of you, how excited are you that you've
made it this far?" Brandon asks and tilts his head.
"I feel like I've had the time of my life here." Tiny
answers, which brings a laugh through the crowd.

"I can agree with that." Alessandro adds.

"I think we all can." Tiny says in her small voice.

"Now Sadie, you've had a lot happen to you over the past few weeks and somehow, you have had not even one vote to evict your designs. How much, does that surprise you?" Brandon tells me.

"Really?" I think out loud. "That really surprises me. Not even one?"

"Not even one." Brandon confirms.

I'm just about star struck by that. Does everyone love my designs or hate them so much, they know they can vote me out at the very end with no problem? Then I remember the girl that works at the shop across from the hospital. She loves my designs and so does everyone else that works there. I decide on the best option as I actually see the girl sitting with her friends at the third row, all wearing a new version of my shirt. On it reads, Seams like Sadie. *Hm. It has a good ring to it.* Brandon gets my surprised face and takes it as an answer to his question.

"Now, I believe this question may determine who gets the majority of the votes tonight: How are you planning to spend the prize money? Has it changed from your original plan?" Brandon asks with such intensity, I become filled with so much passion for my answer. Tiny answers first:

"I am still sticking to my original plan of getting a new barn for the family and possibly another house that's better than our current one. Houses down in the South where I am aren't that expensive anyway." This gets another laugh from the live crowd. "I may also contribute some extra money to these three because of how far we've gone together as a whole."

"Ah. Yes. I see. Anyone else like to answer that?" Brandon asks as he surveys the remaining four of us.

"I would." I raise my hand a little.

"Yes, Sadie?" Brandon prompts me.

"I'd like to of course stick to my original plan, just like Tiny, but at the same time, I'd like to give some money to Skylar and her family because this whole time since her accident, she's never really been voted off the game. She just can't come back to compete because of how faulty her body has been working. I'm not trying to be that one hero that's always thinking about the right thing to do, but I would feel horrible keeping all that money to myself whenever I probably would've been voted off the show way before this if she was still in the game." I explain. The crowd makes an *aweing* sound as I finish.

Lucy explains that she'll probably save the money for later when she goes to college and Alessandro explains how he wants to bring his sister to America from Italy.

"It's really not a bad place at all. She loves it there but I feel like she'll love it more here in America."

"Ah. Thank you all. Everyone, to your stations." Brandon opens his arms out wide and we all rush to our stations. "Here's how it'll work: There will be two rounds: in the first one, you'll have to sew a set of PJs, just like what you're wearing today. Then, America will vote on whose they like better and the losing team will be eliminated. In the second round, the remaining team will split up and have to design a fancy outfit to wear to a dance. The reason I'm telling you the categories now is because you won't get a refill on fabric so use it wisely. Are you ready to play, Fashion on the run: New York?"

"Wait." Lucy yells. "So, this is the season finale?"

"Indeed, it is Miss Davis." Brandon says knowingly.

"Once again, are you ready to play, Fashion on the run: New York?"

"No." Lucy yells again. "Who will be voting on the second round?"

Brandon sighs. "It's part of the fun, my dear. You'll have to find out if you make it to the finals. One last time, are you ready to play Fashion on the run: New York?"

This time we all answer. "Yes."

"Your time, begins, NOW." Brandon exclaims as the PJ category pops up onto the screen.

"What should we do?" Alessandro asks me.

"I've got an idea." I grab the sketch book and pencil laying on the table and sketch out a PJ jumpsuit with long sleeves and pants all attached to the bodice. "You think you can do this?" I show him the sketch pad.

"Sounds good. I'll get the thread in the machine loaded up. You can lay out the fabrics." He orders.

I throw the sketch pad on the desk and pull out the heavy fabric bin stowed under the sewing table where Alessandro sits. I grab some pins and put them in my mouth so I can hold them. I sit on my knees as I search through the fabric bin. I really want to do something simple but to win this round with America's votes, I need something stylish. How is that going to work? I keep rummaging through the bin and find nothing.

"You ok?" Alessandro asks me. "I'm ready for the fabric."

"I can't find anything. If we want to win with America's vote, we'll need something fancy. I can't find anything that looks like it could become 'fancy PJs.'" I tell him.

"We're running out of time. Let me look." He gets out of the chair and kneels down by the fabric bin to search.

"You take my place." I stand up and sit in the sewing chair and make sure everything on the machine is right for the PJ. "I found some flannel. How about we use that to make a shirt and we can top it with golden buttons?"

"Sounds good." I tell him. He hands me the fabric and I start by cutting out the shirt as Alessandro starts cutting out the pants. Once I finish cutting out both sides, I put them together and start stitching an intricate, delicate, line to hold the shirt together. Once I'm done stitching, I hop out of the chair to let Alessandro get in and stitch his pants in with the elastic and special slippers I see sketched out on the sheet of paper. I grab an extra needle that the machine is not using and start on a gold button. I prefer to use a machine to sew, but with buttons, I neatly stitch them onto the flannel shirt so I don't make a mistake. By the time I'm done with the buttons, Alessandro is done with the pants and the slippers. On the outside, the slippers match the outfit with the flannel but on the inside, the slippers have a fluffy cotton material that makes it look a little bit like Santa's beard is coming out of the flannel.

"That looks great. We need to start assembling now." I instruct.

"Do you think you're done?" Brandon says into his microphone. "Since America is voting tonight, we're giving you all thirty extra minutes to complete a *new* set of PJs that you and your partner can both model. Press this button to start your extra time." Brandon motions to the big red button on a little post in the center of the stage.

"What?" The staff bring out one more mannequin for Alessandro and I as I start to panic. "I'll model this outfit. You start on the one for you. I'll go get the button."

"Go. We can have forty-five minutes if you press that button now." Alessandro yells as I'm already on my way to the button.

As I sprint across the stage to the button, I see Tiny is also on her way. I sprint faster because I know I have to win this. She starts sprinting faster too and reaches out for the button when, BAM. I press the button just seconds before Tiny does and a huge buzzer sounds through the big room.

"The first contestant to reach the button, Sadie Benton. Go." Brandon announces as I run back to my section to help Alessandro. He's already cutting.

"Don't we need to measure?" I ask.

"Who has time for that? I'm making it extra baggy so it will fit me no matter what." Alessandro informs me.

"What if it's too big?" I grab the other side of the flannel fabric he's holding.

He looks me in the eye. "Trust me and start cutting the pants." I can't say no to that. I grab the other side of the roll of fabric and start cutting out both sides of the pants.

"Could you sew this together? I'm scared I'll mess the pants up. I'll cut your shirt?" I ask. If I mess a seam up, we're both doomed.

"Sure." I hand Alessandro the fabric and he starts sewing as I continue to cut out the shape of his shirt. After about a good twenty minutes or so, I can hear the sewing machine come to a halt. "Sadie, did you ever think to leave room for the elastic?"

"There's no room?" I start to panic and I feel like I might pass out again.

"We just lost thirty minutes because of you, Sadie." Alessandro glares down on me.

"I didn't mean to. How about I sew the shirt and you can fix the pants?" What if I messed this up for both of us?

"I think I've had enough of your help on the sewing behalf. You can go get ready in your outfit." Alessandro looks down and starts dramatically snipping through a new piece of fabric.

There're so many things I want to say to him right now. *You wouldn't even be here if I didn't choose you for my team. I've sewed lots of pants and haven't messed up like this before.* I take a deep breath in and wheel the mannequin with my outfit on it to the dressing room. If I were in his position, I probably would be angry too. He's just having a moment. I undress out of my PJs and put the new pair of PJs on. They somehow fit perfectly without me needing to fix anything. I feel like it's back to the original day of the auditions. Me trying on clothes that I sewed myself and picking out shoes and accessories to go with my outfit. I find a little plaid beanie and braid my hair to make it look like it's a cold winter's night and I'm wearing the comfiest PJs anyone has ever seen. I think I've accomplished that. I sit on the little dressing room stool and watch what's going on outside the room since I can't go back out with my "big-debut" outfit. The camera is filming Alessandro eighty-five percent of the time so everyone watching can see how much he struggles while under pressure. He cuts and sews so rapidly he has to make little patches of fabric to cover where he ripped the material. I wish I could tell him to slow down and relax but he seems too stressed out and working too quickly that if anyone were to tell him anything, he would do the exact opposite. After another twenty-or-so minutes, he finally finishes with a good seven and a half minutes left so he rushes into the dressing room next to me. I knock on the wall: "You okay, Alessandro?" No response. Then, a little knock.
"We're on in seven minutes." He sounds a little bit more relaxed. "I ripped a few things."
"I saw that."
"Tiny still isn't done yet." He informs me.
"Good to know. You ready?"
"Ready as ever." He replies.

I watch the screen for the next five minutes as Tiny and Lucy are both running around the place and trying on new outfits and making, literally, last minute fixer-uppers. Finally, the time comes and Brandon calls us out with our teammate two at a time to show off our outfits and give us a slight interview sort of thing. Tiny and Lucy get called out first, wearing pants that have small snags on the bottom. They run the interview swiftly and walk back into their station as Brandon calls out Alessandro and I. We walk out of the dressing room right on cue and show off our outfits to the audience as we walk to the chairs next to Brandon.

"I have one question for the two of you, how did you like working as a team, knowing that you'll either have to compete against each other or lose because the other one of you made a mistake?" Brandon eyes Alessandro.

"Well," Alessandro starts before I can answer anything. "It would really disappoint me if Sadie had made a mistake that caused both of us to lose. I probably would just say goodbye and leave." Alessandro chuckles.

"And if you didn't lose?" Brandon prompts.

"Then bummer. Sadie carried me all this way but now her backpack broke and I have to walk myself. I would really have to keep in mind that in the next half, I'll have to work really hard." Alessandro gets a good laugh out of everyone with his analogies.

"What about you Sadie?" Brandon asks me.

"Well, it depends if you want me to be completely honest or not." I laugh. "If I *am* being honest, I would just cry in my room for a few days and get myself enrolled in school so I'd have something better to think about and to focus my attention on. I like my on-set teacher, but I'd be ready to be back at a real school".

"What about if you do win?" Brandon asks me again.

"Well, I'll then realize that my backpack broke. In other words, I'd know that either way, one of us is going to win so it's technically a win for both of us." I try to use one of Alessandro goofy phrases.

"Well, thank you for your *honest* answers, Sadie." Brandon giggles. "Well then, it is now the moment everyone has been waiting for. Please pull out your phones and vote for the team you'd like to move on. Tiny, Lucy, please come join Sadie and Alessandro at the front of the stage."

As I walk to the front of the stage, I see what looks like a million little lights from everyone's cellphones lighting up as they vote this huge decision that will either fill me up or completely deflate me. After, officially, the longest three minutes of my life, Brandon announces the voting session ends in thirty seconds. As I stand at the front of the stage, I can sort of tell who people have voted for. I see a few faces glaring me down and a few that are gazing majestically at Tiny and Lucy, an obvious vote for them. Then, I see others who smile at me brightly or give me a thumbs up when I meet their gaze. Finally, a staff member walks out of the backstage door with a silky white envelope that's sealed with a red ribbon. It reminds me of Mark's and Peter's middle school graduation certificates. Although then it only meant good news, not a decision that could change my life for better or worse. Brandon *slowly* opens the envelope, only to add to my enormous pile of suspense.

"The team, that will be moving on to the finals is," a thunderous drumroll erupts from the audience. "Sadie Benton and Alessandro Cipresso."

Chapter 29

I leap into Alessandro's arms and squeeze him as we jump up and down, up and down. After a few minutes of that, we let go and walk over to Tiny and Lucy. "Congratulations." Lucy says as she hugs me. I give her the hugest hug back and try my best to help her feel better.

"You guys did a great job." Alessandro reassures them.

"Just not good enough." Tiny mumbles.

Then, Alessandro does something I would've never thought he'd done in a million years. He goes over to Tiny, stands right in front of her and gives her a small peck on the lips. Tiny looks up and stares at him, bewildered. Lucy and I look at each other for a quick second and then stare right back at Tiny and Alessandro.

"Wow. In the first year of F.O.T.R, we get a full-on show. All right you two, Tiny has to get going backstage." Brandon announces. After Tiny and Lucy walk backstage, Brandon continues. "Later tonight, we'll do a final interview with Tiny, Lucy, and the second-place winner. But WOW. Alessandro, will there be any dates with Tiny in your future?"

"I just did it for the show." Alessandro winks at the camera, only I know that he didn't do it for that reason.

"Well alright then. Let's get to the final, and most intense round of the F.O.T.R show. "Let's do this." Brandon yells, loud enough for everyone to hear, even without his microphone. The glass walls that separated Tiny's station and mine falls down. Then, all twelve walls pop back up into place and Brandon instructs us to get back to our original stations. Alessandro and I hug as we walk off to our separate stations.

"Good luck, Sadie." Alessandro whispers to me, quiet enough that his microphone couldn't pick it up.

"Good luck, Alessandro." I whisper back.
"This last and final round of FOTR is going to be based after," The screen glows presenting our topic of clothing. "An outfit to be presented on the front cover of Vogue. Since we have an audience, you only have two hours to complete both a male and female outfit. Does that sound like something you two can do?"
Well, two hours. An hour for the female outfit, probably a dress, and an hour for the male outfit probably a sweatshirt and some ripped jeans. That sounds ok. I think. I'm already bubbling with ideas for the female outfit but still have no idea for the male outfit.
"Are you two ready," Brandon starts as the audience joins in as the chorus. "For the final, round, of, FOTR?"
"Yes." Alessandro and I both shout as the audience applauds while we rush to our sewing stations.
I immediately start rummaging through the fabric bin to find the fabrics to complete my design. I was thinking of a short, knee-high dress that has a golden V-neck collar with half of the dress white and the other half black. I could wear it with some black heels and a white flower hairclip. I knew right at that instant that was my design. For only my third time this season, I looked through the pattern magazine to get one for a little dress. I had to guarantee myself that I wouldn't mess up and a pattern was just how to do it. I looked through the book until I found a little dress pattern that matched the shape of my design. I ripped the pattern out of the book and laid it out on the ground.

I sat on my knees as I carefully pinned the black fabric to the pattern where I can cut. I slowly cut out the black piece of fabric using the pattern and set it by the sewing machine. I then took the white silky fabric and pinned it to the same pattern to get an even shape on both sides of the dress. Once I got that cut out, I laid the two sides of the dress next to each other, making them overlap a little bit on the inside. I folded them together to make the form of a body and stitched a nice even seam right down the middle, as the pattern instructed. I unfolded the dress once I finished sewing them together and held it out in front of me. *Yes.* I completely nailed it. I hang the dress up on the mannequin and cut off a few loose strings. Then, for the challenge: the boy outfit. Alessandro was always there to help me with this part but I'll have to face this part on my own today.

I go back to the bin and search through the rest of the fabrics that I hadn't looked through yet. After looking through the fabrics I just decided to go with an extra shiny black fabric for a jacket and bow tie and a silk white fabric that I'll use for and undershirt. I also just decided to use a plain black fabric for the pants. *I think that sounds like a pretty decent outfit for a male.* I comfort myself as best as I can.

I draw out the design on a piece of scratch paper because I'm much more likely to forget this outfit plan while I search for a pattern. After I sketch a brief design, I grab the big pattern book and look for a shirt pattern, a jacket type pattern, and some pants for a man. Once I find all three, I rip them out as fast as I can and start cutting and pinning, cutting and pinning until everything is neatly cut out just as I want them to be.

I look at the big clock on the screen, *eighteen minutes*. I start speeding things up. I quickly stitch together the simple white shirt and black pants but hesitate before I start sewing the jacket. This is what everyone will look at on this outfit. I pause and start sewing on the simple bowtie instead. I keep getting that feeling that I'm going to mess something up and since there's just the bowtie and the jacket left, it has to be the jacket. I finish the bowtie a lot faster than I wanted to. Why did I choose the jacket? I look at the clock again and realize how little time I have left. *Stop procrastinating.* I yell at myself in my head. I decide to just go for it and grab the pieces and stitch together the jacket in a neat intricate pattern of steps: Sleeve one onto side B, sleeve two onto side A. I stitch the sleeves on and make a little cuff at the end, remembering some of my dad's outfits he used to wear to work. I finish sewing the cuffs and the seams at the ends of the jacket. I carefully place the outfit on the second mannequin and smooth out the wrinkles. I grab the scissors and start snipping off little threads that hang loose from the jacket and shirt. Then all of a sudden, I see the clock in the corner of my eye. Thirty seconds until I have to get to the dressing room.

I stop smoothing the creases in the jacket and rush to my first mannequin. I wheel my mannequin into my dressing room and start undressing myself and the mannequin at the same time. Pajama bottoms off, dress on. I put the dress on and pull the zipper up the back of my dress. Carrie rushes into my room through the door that opens up to backstage with a brush in her hand and a makeup brush in her mouth. She waves at me in a way with her eyes since her hands and her mouth are full. She rushes over to me and sets the things down on a little stool in the dressing room and helps me zip up my dress.

"Looking good." She gives me a thumbs up.

"Thanks." I smile. She grabs her brush that she brought with her and runs it through my tangled hair.

"What did you do with your hair?" She asks in astonishment at my tangled mess.

"I might've been pulling on it a little, tiny, tiny, little bit." I give her an indication of how small with my fingers. She rolls her eyes at me, although I'm sure she understood the stress I was in when I picked at my hair. She sets the brush down and gets to work with the blower brush. I grab some black heels off the shoe rack and a white pearl hair clip too. "Could you put this in my hair too?" I ask Carrie. Her eyes covered in extreme amounts of eyeshadow meet my gaze and she smiles at me.

"Stop stressing out. You'll do great." She tells me.

"I'll keep telling myself that." I mutter. She puts the pearl clip into my hair and fastens it with a little, almost-invisible, hair tie. She grabs her makeup brush and gets to work on my face while I smooth out the dress nervously. Through the bristles of the makeup brush, I can see my reflection in the mirror. The dress looks back at me with a beautiful golden strip across the middle and black on one side, white on the other. It feels like me. There's always a little bit of me that feels incapable at times but at the same time I have a side of me that feels strong and able to do anything. But then that gold line in the middle is where I usually stand. Enough doubt about myself that makes me powerful through all the challenges life throws at me. That gold line is where I stand with Marie and Addy on either side of me and Thew following closely behind. My brothers are there with my aunt and mom, my dad slowly faded in the background. Carrie finishes with my makeup and I feel ready to achieve anything. I've got this. Carrie gives me a thumbs up and turns me to face the door where I'll walk out to show the world who I really am.

Chapter 30

Brandon's microphone turns on once he gets the "ok" signal and calls Alessandro and I out one by one to show off the outfit we've created. Brandon first calls out the models for the second outfit. My model is this cute boy with brown hair and green eyes who even strides across the stage, giving America the look that could win over anyone. Next Alessandro's female model walks out wearing an exquisite looking gold dress with a sparkly gold trail that follows about five or six feet behind the blonde-haired blue-eyed girl. After the models walk backstage, Brandon calls out Alessandro and I and we walk out simultaneously, me wearing my black, white, and gold dress and Alessandro wearing a long sleeve white shirt with metallic silver overalls. I walk out in my heels, feeling confident as ever, and give my hair a flip to the audience. Everyone *oooohhs* and *ahhhhs* at my hair flip and my design as I do my semi-professional catwalk back down the aisle. As Alessandro and I walk to the director's chars sitting in the center of the stage, we exchange a glance and a small smile. I hoist myself into the tall director's chair and wait for Brandon to come join Alessandro and I. He sits in the remaining director's chair that's angled in a way so that he's facing us and the audience.

"All right. Are you guys ready to vote?" He asks the audience as soon as he gets himself into the chair. "You can pull out your phone and use the same website as last time to vote for the one, and final winner of Fashion on the Run: New York." Everyone cheers loudly as Brandon reads everyone the website one more time in case they forgot. "While they vote, I have just a few more questions for you two, if you wouldn't mind."

"Sure thing." Alessandro replies.

"Of course." I nod.

"Who do you think is going to win this very first season of FOTR?"

"That's a hard one." Alessandro says automatically.

"Agreed." I nod my head once more. "We're both really great competitors, if you don't mind me saying." I wink at the audience and get a few seconds of laughter.

"True. We both *really* want this as well." Alessandro says.

"Either way, do you two think it'll be a good win either way?" Brandon prompts.

"Yes, of course." I blurt. "Alessandro has been one of my few friends during this game and we've seemed to work together very well. I'm so happy I met him through this experience".

"Sadie has been an outstanding partner, considering what we've both gone through during this season." Alessandro starts. "First, her parents split and she has to straight up move out of her home with little notice. Then, she witnesses the tragic event with Skylar, her greatest competitor. Next, another tragic accident involving herself with a crazy lady and a spider. Finally, she's here today, looking even more stunning than ever before, after kicking butt in challenge after challenge. Right, audience?" I blush a little at the "stunning" part.

"Sadie has been through a lot." Brandon agrees. "How do you feel right now, Sadie, living this moment? Is it a dream or a nightmare for you with all that has happened?"

"That's also a hard question." I breathe out. "It has been a ton of stuff, all happening in such a short amount of time. It doesn't necessarily feel like a dream or a nightmare, or even reality really. I just feel like I've figured out how to process things that are going on more quickly and they seem like less of a big deal now, if that makes sense."

"Ah. One last question, specifically for Sadie." Brandon
announces. "Do you have anyone to get back to if you
win the prize money and return home?"
I feel my cheeks go red. All of a sudden, the lights feel
too hot again, like the first time I set foot upon this stage.
My lungs squeeze together tightly and I can't breathe.
Tonight's the night. *Today* is three months from then.
The memories fly back to me in a gust of wind that no
one else seems to feel but me. The gust knocks me out of
my chair and I'm on the floor. The one boy I can't stop
thinking about. Thew. My Thew. Has he moved on? Is
there another girl out there that he's found more
interesting than me? Maybe he'll be having the time of
his life in just ten hours from now, dancing with another
girl in a pretty gown with pretty hair and pretty
shoes…the gust keeps blowing. I blink my eyes once and
realize there was no storm, no powerful gust of wind that
knocked me out of my seat. I'm sitting perfectly still,
Brandon and Alessandro awaiting my response. I feel
exhausted. I can't move on. What was the question? My
mouth does the talking and not my brain.
"What exactly are you asking me?" I say in a humorous
tone that I didn't feel coming. The crowd laughs and I
begin to feel all eyes being taken away from their phones
to directly stare at me. I'm in the FOTR theatre. In front
of a crowd. On the finale episode. "Of course, I have
someone waiting for me." I finally realize where I am and
continue with the humorous tone.
Brandon looks like he had just gotten the gust of wind.
Probably from my sudden change of emotion. "Well,
that's all I needed to know. Shall we read the votes?" He
says looking puzzled at me.

I decide not to answer that question to try to prevent the word vomit that could potentially come from my mouth at this point. Alessandro does the talking for me. "Let's do it." As soon as Alessandro says those words, Carrie and his stylist walk out wearing snazzy gold outfits and oversized, shiny, jet-black belts. Each of them holds a matching sparkly gold envelope. Carrie meets my gaze and gives me a small thumbs up under the envelope. "You've got this." She mouths. I smile back and find myself staring at the envelope like it's covered in diamonds. Carrie walks to the front of the stage and starts talking into her gold microphone in her other hand. Her otherwise curly brown hair was straightened to form long waves down her back. She ditched her black cat eye glasses for her fifteen minutes of fame.
"Thank you all so very much for joining us on this very exciting morning." She says in a voice that I know is definitely not natural, but rehearsed over and over about a hundred times to fit the vibe of this moment. "In this envelope, I'll reveal who has one the very first season of Fashion on the Run: New York. This will determine not only who has won the prize money and the first season of this show, but also a guarantee of this person's future in fashion. Before the big reveal, I'll let my fellow stylist say a few words." She moves to stand off to the side of the stage so Alessandro' stylist can take the lead. Alessandro's stylist walks up to the front of the stage holding the other envelope.

"I'd first just like to give a huge round of applause to all of our FOTR competitors, Lucy Davis, Ivy Smith, Victoria Johnson, Clara Campbell, Trinity Brown, Emily Garcia, Chloe King, Stella Wilson, and Autumn Hill. I'd then like to take a small moment out of respect for Skylar Jones, for originally coming out here to compete in this fashion competition, and for ending up competing in an even more important battle, one for her life. Our thoughts and prayers are with Skylar and her family as she continues to battle. Lastly, a standing ovation for our final two competitors, Sadie Benton and Alessandro Cipresso, who have made it this far and still manage to keep hope and continue to be inspired."

Enormous applause erupts from the crowd. Whistles chime in the thunderous applause. Carrie than walks up to the head of the stage to open her envelope and announce the winner. This is the moment I have been waiting for. This is the moment everyone that's in this theatre has been waiting for. The golden envelope.

Carrie holds the envelope at waist level and makes it a dramatic scene as she rips the little sticky part off the top. She lets the sticky part fall to the floor in a golden swirl as she slowly pulls out a velvet note card.

"The winner, of this year's season of FOTR," Carrie begins with a smile widening on her face with every word. "Sadie Benton."

There's a huge pause. Then finally, the loudest applause I'd ever heard in my *life*, begins. Yelling and shouting of excitement. I see people standing up out of their chairs and clapping for me. A panel above me in the celling opens up and white, gold, and silver confetti rain down on me. I stick my hands out on either side of me and feel the confetti come down like little flakes of snow. *I won. This can't be happening. I really won.* Out of the corner of my eye, I see the screens on the left and right of the theatre light up in pink and huge white letters roll across the screen with my name.

"One more surprise, Sadie." Brandon begins.

"Really? I'm not sure there's anything else I can handle." I laugh as the confetti continues to fall, not just on me now, but over the whole theatre.

"Since you won FOTR, you have everyone's respect right now. All those online trolls and haters know that you are the winner. You did this, Sadie. Is there one wish that you have left? Something that we can do for you as our first ever winner of FOTR? We have space here at the studio if you want to throw a big party or we can bring in our designers to help you customize a logo for your fashion business? Anything right now, Sadie. Do you have any ideas?" Brandon asks. The theatre doesn't go quiet but it definitely settles down a little to hear my response. I think for not even a second because I know exactly what I want. This is what I ultimately came here for. Not for New York to love me and give me all the fame I could imagine, but for my family. For my *home*. New York isn't my home and it never will be no matter how much I feel like I belong here.

"I do have one, teensy tiny request." I admit to Brandon.

"Go on." He looks at me with a questionable expression.

"I need to whisper this to you to keep it a surprise." I lean into to Brandon's ear and we both put our hands over our mics so nobody can hear. "There is this one thing happening later tonight, back in my hometown. It's a little dance and it starts at eight. Do you think someone could get me there in time?" I whisper, hopefully.
"I think that's manageable." Brandon whispers back to me with a wink. Then the hugs come. Mark, Peter, Mom, and Aunt Kara have made it down to the stage by now and are taking turns squeezing me so hard that I can barely breathe.
"Miss Sadie, what did you whisper to Brandon? And will you be staying in New York for your fashion business?" A reporter, I never even saw walk in, holds a microphone to my mouth.
"Um. Well. What I whispered is a surprise and of course, I'll always come *back* to New York. It's like a home away from home for me." I answer.
"If you're planning to come back to New York, where are you planning on going?" A new reporter asks me.
"Tell me, what will you do with all this money?" Another reporter asks. More and more reporters come up to me and over all the voices, I hear one. Brandon is addressing me.
"Sadie, Sadie. Ronald is waiting for you outside." Brandon shouts above the crowds of reporters. Then he leans in and whispers, "if you want to make it back home in time for the dance, you'll need to leave now."
I need to leave. I look at the crowd of reporters waiting anxiously for a response I didn't even hear the question to. How will I get out of here?

"I have this really great competitor next to me who got this far into FOTR with his amazing talent. How about you ask him a few questions?" I point to Alessandro, who stands away from the crowd, trying not to steal my thunder. As on cue, all the reporters rush over to Alessandro and he gives me a huge grin when he realizes what I did. I give him a thumbs up and turn around to face Aunt Kara and the rest of my family.

"Looks like I'm going back home for the dance. Are you guys coming too?" I squeal with excitement.

"We can't, Sadie. This is for you and not us. The crew members got a hold of Ronald and he's taking you back." Aunt Kara answers.

"Will you guys be okay when I'm there?" I ask them frantically.

"We'll be fine." Peter answers. "You've got a car to catch, so go. Don't worry about us."

I turn to run out the door but Alessandro catches my dress and pulls me back with the trail of reporters behind him.

"Hey, I managed to get this for you in case you didn't win or in this case, as a celebratory gift." His stylist stands next to him and pulls out the newest version smart phone. "Consider it a gift from me to you, alright? Just in case you forget me. Oh, and don't break it." Alessandro laughs.

"Alessandro. You didn't have-" I get interrupted by a big hug from Alessandro.

"Just also promise me, no more spiders."

"Sounds manageable." I quote Brandon. We both laugh and he lets go of me.

"Bye, Sadie."

"Bye, Alessandro." I wave at everyone on stage one last time before I run to the door. One last time before I exit, I look at the crowd, eyes following me wherever I go. "I couldn't have done this without you guys. Thank you so much for choosing me." I blow a kiss and take my microphone off. Then, I burst through the door.

Chapter 31

When I get outside the studio, I take one last glance
through the closing door behind me. I see all my fans
waving at me and cheering my name and Alessandro
staring back at me. I look for the black limo but see
nothing in the reserved parking lot for cast and crew. I do
see a big black van with an even longer back than a limo.
This must be my ride. I think. I walk up to the window
and Ronald waves me into the door that slowly opens for
me. I grab a handlebar at the top of the car and hoist
myself into the vehicle.
"Hey, princess. Great job out there." he says,
"Thanks." I respond.
"Your Aunt Kara wouldn't like me telling you this but
she had this customized for you as soon as you got into
the competition. She thought you might need to be on the
road more when you won this thing. There's a closet in
the back and a little room where you can spend your time.
It'll be a pretty long drive from here to your school so
make yourself at home."
"Aunt Kara." I mumble to myself in astonishment.
"Thank you so much for being here, Ronald."
I walk back down the little corridor in the car and see my
dressing room door on the left and my personal room on
the right. I walk into my little room first. I open the door
and find the predictable Aunt Kara flair everywhere.
Nothing less would be acceptable for her.

It's not a small living space but about the size of an average kids' bedroom. It has a small white desk with a little cord to plug my phone in. It also has a fuzzy white beanbag on the floor, propped up right in front of a little twenty by twenty TV bolted into the car. The floor of this room has white carpet to match my desk and beanbag. In the very back of the room is a small bed, just long enough for me to fit in, with little posh pillows strewn across it. I plug my phone in and sit on my bed. I look around me, amazed at everything happening right now. I feel numb and then I feel the car start to move as I look through the black tinted windows out at New York.

For a bit I just lay on my bed, thinking about what just happened in my life. *I won FOTR. I won against all eleven other competitors.* Laying on my bed doesn't last long though with all my excitement. I sit up just in time to see The Empire State building out in the distance about a mile away. I see the huge complex that my aunt lives in. As we keep driving, I see the little alleyway with the shops and restaurants that my aunt and I went shopping at one day. As much as my home isn't here, it will always be another safe place for me. We keep driving for a few more minutes until I see the little signs signifying that we're headed out of New York and into a different state. I walk out of my little room and head to my dressing room to get into more comfortable clothes and settle in for the ride. When I walk in, it reminds me of a smaller version of my closet back at Aunt Kara's house. Except way smaller.

Pink walls and clothes hanging from all angles. I walk around a little corner and get some sweatpants and a cropped T-shirt with FOTR written on the front. I take out my hair in the little star mirror and put my heels up with the rest of the shoes. My hair bobs out of Carrie's braided-bun style in little ring curls that only fancy ladies would've had in the Victorian era. I set the pearl hair clip down on the dresser below the star mirror. I lay my dress down in a cabinet labeled,

For Winning Dress ONLY

Aunt Kara's writing. I gently stroke the dress with my fingers. *I did it.* Today is a day I will always remember. I walk back to my room with a now uncontrollable grin. *I won all of FOTR. I can get our house back. I get a private ride back home to see Thew. And, I even get a new phone from Alessandro. Best. Day. Ever.*

I settle into the little bean-bag chair and grab the remote that was laying on top of it. I switch the channel to FOTR and watch Alessandro having the time of his life answering all the bazillion questions the reporters are asking him. I switch to a different channel and on it is the news with Jamie Jones, famous reporter on *all* things fashion. She's in the FOTR studio and interviewing Mark.

"Do you feel proud of your sister right now?" She asks Mark.

"Of course. I've always known that she's had a knack for this sort of thing."

"Did you ever think she would get this far into FOTR and even win the whole show?"

"Well, you can never doubt her."

"Now, what is she up to now? What was the surprise that she whispered to Brandon?"

"That's for Sadie to answer." Mark answers, now flustered with all the personal questions.

Peter walks up. "Yo yo ladies." He says to the camera lens. Classic Peter.

Now it's Jamie's turn to be flustered. "You're…Sadie's other brother, right? Potter?"

Peter freezes, "It's Peter."

"Of course, of course. Sorry. Do you feel proud of Sadie right now?"

"Duh. Who isn't?" Peter answers coolly.

Jamie's facial expression changes dramatically and she has a flirty look on her face now. Ah. Just another classic reporter with another classic Peter.

I switch the channel again to find a different reporter interviewing my mom and Aunt Kara. Well, mostly Aunt Kara. With Aunt Kara's big personality, there isn't much that my mom has to do or say, just the occasional nod or yes.

I switch the channel again and find yet another reporter interviewing audience members and previous contestants. Tiny talks for a while about how much fun it was to be on the show and how she's proud of me for my accomplishments. Then, in the middle of one of her stretched out country expressions, Alessandro runs up to her with a trail of reporters and lifts her off the ground and into his arms. Out of all my time being around those two, how did I not notice the obvious glances they pass back and forth with each other sooner? It's kind of funny how Alessandro holds her in his arms because Tiny is just a tad bit taller than him. I laugh to myself as I watch. I have to admit they *are* pretty cute together.

I set the remote down and grab my new phone from the desk. I bring it back down to the beanbag with me and try to get the phone open. It doesn't work. *Come on phone. Open. It's me, Sadie.* I try to think of a six-digit code. My birthday? Nope. The day I moved to New York? Nope. But wait. I type in today's date and it lets me in. The day I won FOTR. When it takes me to the home screen, all my apps are already downloaded. Alessandro had to have this programmed long before. Or, he had Rick's tech help. Genius. Both of them. I open my text messages. I hit the button for the group chat with Thew, Addy, and Marie. But then again, I pause. I switch to the group chat with just Addy and Marie. For some reason, I don't feel like texting Thew right now. What if he already has date and he's out getting his outfit or something right now. Definitely not a good time. I text Addy and Marie and get immediate responses.

Me: Hey guys. You'll never believe it.

Marie: We know. We've been glued to the TV all morning long. Congrats.

Me: It's not just that…

Addy: SKIP THE DRAMATIC INTRO JUST TELL US THE NEWSSSSSSS

Me: Alright, fine. I'm in the car right now on the way to the school. I'll be there for the dance tonight.

Addy: WAIT! WHAT? YOU COULD'VE TOLD US THAT LIKE EIGHT MINUTES AGO

Me: Sorry, sorry. I was watching TV.

Marie: In the car? Or are you watching YouTube waiting to get in the car?

Me: In the car my aunt let me use. You guys remember my aunt from that playdate we had when we were three with the whole cast of Paw Patrol that showed up and the three-decker cake…when it wasn't even my birthday?

Addy: Oh yeah. Makes sense now.

Marie: You're so lucky to have an Aunt like that. I can't believe we get to see you again tonight. It feels like it's been forever.
Me: Same. Do you guys have dates this year?
Addy: I got a date with DJ board.
Me: You're going to be amazing.
Addy: Sure hope so. I've been practicing too :)
Marie: I just have a little date with someone from my math class. We just sit next to each other and he asked me out as friends. Does Thew know you're coming back? He'll be thrilled.
Me: No. Not yet. I was worried he would already have a date this year and I didn't want to bug him...
Marie: Of course not. He sits at our table with a few of his guy friends. He tries to talk about other things, but it always ends up leading to you and how he misses you. I don't think he likes you Sadie, I think he loves you. Text him now and tell him.
Addy: WAIT. DON'T TEXT HIM. MAKE IT A SURPRISE AND SHOW UP OUT OF NOWHERE.
Marie: Maybe. That's actually not a bad idea.
Me: You want me to wait to text him?
Addy: Don't text him at all. Just show up.
Marie: Tell whoever's driving you to pull up around the back of the school. That's where the snack bar is. Then you can text me when you're five minutes away and I'll tell Mathew to get a snack. How's that?
Addy: Perf. LET'S DO THIS.
Me: Sounds good to me. Can't wait. I'll go tell my driver, Ronald, what's up. TTYL
Addy: Toddles.
Marie: Bye bye.

I turn off my phone and tuck it safely in my back pocket where it won't get lost. Or broken. I walk out of my room and open the little door to the driver and passenger seats.

"Hey princess. Need anything? There're snacks in the back if you want some."

"Oh no, I'm fine. Thank you. I was just wondering if you could pull around the back of the school instead of the front. My two best friends have a plan that requires me to arrive at the back of the school." I shrug.

"Sure, sure. No problem. I'll remind you thirty minutes before so you have time to get dressed."

"Thank you so much."

"Sure princess."

I close up his door and walk back into my room. I lay on bed, gazing out the window. Who would've guessed today, of all days, would be a good day for a long road trip? I feel my phone buzz and I look at the screen. *Dad.* I hesitantly press the *answer* button and wait for his voice.

"Hey, honey. Congratulations." He says warmly through the phone.

"Um, thanks, I guess?"

"Hey, I know it's been a lot for you recently with the move and everything. I just wanted to call-"

I stop him midsentence. "It's been a lot for me?" I yell into the phone. "It was all because of you and you know that. I've hardly heard from you in all these years and you call to tell me what? About how it's been *hard* for me?" All my bottled-up anger explodes.

"Sadie, I know how you feel." He tries to reassure me.

"No, you don't. *You* chose to leave us. You'd never know how it feels to be left alone without warning."

"I didn't leave you on purpose, Sadie. It was out of my control."

"It was never out of your control because you *chose* that for yourself and for the rest of your *family.*" Tears well up in my eyes.

"You won't get it for a long time, Sadie. I had to leave you guys for your safety, not because I didn't want you anymore."

"So, you think about us? All the time?" I ask him as the tears dangerously threaten to spill out of my eyes.

"Of course, I do, Sadie. Every day. I would never leave you guys out of my own choice. Never. Something was happening that I needed to take care of immediately."

His sentence shocks me into almost silence. "I'm-I'm sorry, Dad." I stutter. "I didn't mean to yell at you. I just don't understand."

He stops me. "No, Sadie. I should be apologizing. I'll see you very soon. Love you."

"What?" I say, exasperated, into the phone. *He'll see me very soon?* The phone beeps as he hangs up and leaves me to my thoughts. I get under the covers and drift off into a much-needed sleep, many unanswered questions swimming around in my head.

Chapter 32

"Hey, princess. Wakey wakey." Ronald says over the load speaker.

"Humbugo..." I yawn. I sit up and wipe the sleep from my eyes. Still a little dazed from everything that happened earlier.

"I'm stopped for gas. We're at the thirty-minute mark right here, K?"

"Thanks." I yawn again. He closes my door and exits the room. I look out the window at the gas station and see many eyes on the car. This type of transport isn't usually found around here. I get up off of the bed.

Me: Thirty-minutes

Addy: Great. Marie and I just got here. We came early to help set up and get my booth ready.

Me: Sounds good. See ya'll soon.

Marie: You sound like you're from the country.

Me: Learned from the best. See you soon.

I head out into my dressing room to find a dress to wear to the dance. There're some pretty pink dresses and a single short purple one with a ballerina skirt. As I look through them, none of them seem like something I would wear to the dance. They're all beautiful though. I keep searching through the dresses until I reach the very last one. The green dress I wore for one of the first episodes on FOTR. The one that Thew likes. But not the same one as last time. The one I wore on the show was a short, tight fitted dress. This one is the same exact dress, but altered in a way so that there's no more sleeves but a white crystal that connects from my neck to the dress, holding it up. It also has a longer skirt that's still tight fitted, but cut a little at the bottom so one of my legs can be seen as I walk. *It's perfect, Aunt Kara strikes again.*

I take the dress off the hanger and carefully pull it on. I stand before the mirror, just as I did hours before, smoothing out the creases and playing with my hair making little knots. I'll have to brush it out sooner than later. I grab some pearly white heels and the white hairclip that I wore earlier and put them both on. I decide to leave my hair out after brushing it and just place the clip on the side. After a while of smoothing out my dress, I head back to my room and sit on the bed.

Marie texts me that the dance just started. She sends me a video of Addy at her DJ booth and a selfie of her and Andrew, her math date. I turn and look out the window. I feel a great surge of happiness, bigger than the one I felt when I won FOTR. I see the little food court with Ice with the Cream and Mason's Cakes. I'm that close to home. As we drive by, I feel the happiness of all the days I went to Ice with the Cream with Thew and all the time I spent before and after school at Mason's Cakes. *I'm home. I'm finally here.* The streets are empty compared to an average New York day, although there are more cars on the road than usual. I put my phone into a little gold handbag to keep with me. Knowing that I'm only minutes away from the school, I hear Marie's ringtone buzz, most likely signifying that she told Thew to get a snack. I decide to go out of my room and sit in the passenger's seat with Ronald for the remainder of the trip.

"You excited?" Ronald asks me.

"More than ever. I can't believe I'm really here right now. Thank you so much. You'll never know how thankful I am to have you."

"Anytime, princess. Your Aunt Kara is like family to me and you are too."

I start to point out all the small things I remember from special times along the way. The park where Dad was trying to teach Mark and Peter to play basketball, but I kept taking the ball and running all the way across the park to get them to chase me. Then, the neighborhood where I've spent many a night rolled out in a sleeping bag watching the stars with Addy and Marie. Next, the more recent one where I see the sewing store that I like to shop at when Mark gets out of school early enough to take me there. Finally, I see the school. There's a huge banner strung across the doors to the gym, smack dab in the front of the school announcing the fall dance. As I drive by in my VIP car, I see all the seventh and eighth grader pairs turn to stare at me. I specifically see Brianna in the center of the crowd, gaping, that for once, all eyes are not on her. Ronald continues to pull around the front until he reaches the fire lane near the back of the gym. "You got it from here?"

I nod and give him a small kiss on the cheek. "You will seriously never know how thankful I am for this."

He presses a button that opens the door and releases a few steps out of the car. *I didn't notice that before.* I wave at him and he closes the doors, then he goes to park at the back lot. I look around. I think I'm at the snack bar, but I don't see Thew yet.

Me: Here. Where is the snack bar? I'm at the fire lane.

Marie: Yay! Just walk a little bit farther down and make a hard right. Student government is selling the snacks and drinks at a little fold out table. It shouldn't be hard to miss.

Me: Kk.

Looking down at my phone, I follow Marie's instructions for the straightaway and start to hear music. *Make a hard right.* I turn myself and spin right into someone's chest. "Ow." My clip falls out of my hair and onto the floor.

"Let me get that for you." Says a familiar voice. He
bends down to pick up the clip. He starts to stand back up
until he sees my face. "Sadie?"
"Thew." We stare into each other's eyes for a minute.
"You're here? How? How did you get here-"
I press two fingers to his mouth to make him stop talking.
"I think I owe you a little something, don't I?" Before he
can respond, I press my lips into his and feel a warm
sensation spreading through my entire body. He puts his
hands on my waist and I wrap my arms around his neck.
Warm tingles run through me from all directions and
down my spine. I stand on my tippy toes and run my
hands through his long, black hair. I release my toes and
stand back on my normal level.
"I've missed you." I say, staring into his gleaming eyes.
"Have you ever done that before?" He asks curiously,
with a humorous glint in his eyes.
"No, why?" I tease back, grabbing his hand.
"Shall we?" He nods to the door entering the gym.
"Let's do this."

END OF BOOK ONE

AKNOWLEDGEMENTS

I want to start off by thanking God, the creator of all things. He helped to guide me through this process of writing and well, through life in general. Thank you for everything that you do.

Next, my family! Thanks for encouraging me to keep this book going and to turn it into something when all I wanted to do was play video games. I will forever thank you guys for that. Specifically, thank you Mom for being the world's greatest Mom. I never could have made this book without you teaching me and encouraging me and always reading to me from the very start of my life. It encouraged a passion for reading and writing. Thank you also for rereading my book and for handling the tedious process of making sure I didn't repeat words or forget a period. I have so many more words to say but to sum it up, I love you so much! Thanks, Dad, for always being the one to give me a hug after a long day of writing and knowing that I needed to get outside and see the sun every once in a while. That always helped me to get a fresh start for my mind and to come up with great ideas for my story. Of course, thanks V for always being the happiness I needed to complete this book. You could always tell when I was grumpy and couldn't think of an idea, so you'd put on the BEST dance shows ever to inspire me. Never be embarrassed to show your talent to the world. You're great at everything you do!

Also, thank you so much to my great aunt for being the inspiration for this book. Ever since I got in touch with you over COVID, I've admired your creativity and positivity in everything you do! You taught me the secrets of sewing and have given me, literally the best, handmade gifts *ever*. Love you lots!

 I'd also like to thank Dalton Tringali for all of your help too! I couldn't have figured out how to get this book out to stores, let alone figuring out how to self-publish, without you. I'm so lucky to have met you and have no words to describe how thankful I am for your help.

Lastly, but most definitely not least, I'd LOVE to thank Lauren Christopher for teaching me not only the basics of writing, but copyediting, storytelling, and so much more. I FOR SURE would not have been able to do this without your guidance. Thank you for always supporting me and for continuing to be my mentor through this long process. Fourth-grade me through seventh-grade me thank you for helping to make this all possible.

Oh wait! One more! Thank **you** so so so very much for seeing this book and picking it up off of the shelf at the library or bookstore or just buying it off of Amazon. Authors are important, but to have the title as an author, we need the readers. Let your mind soar and never stop reading!

Love,
Olivia